I0575127

Collector's Edition of:

"The Eidetic Evidence"

by

Kyle VanDuzer

Prologue

Obituaries

July 29, 2002

Jacklyn Kay (Jackie) Krause Casey 1970-2002
Seattle - Jacklyn Kay (Jackie) Krause Casey, 32, died
July 27, 2002 at her home, Seattle, Wa.
She was born April 19, 1970 in Seattle, to Jason Lee
and Anna Jo (Bechard) Krause. She married Melvin
Ray (Mel) Casey October 12th, 1996, in Seattle.
They are the parents of Aaron Jason Casey, who
was born January 17th, 2000, in Seattle, WA. Both
Mel and Aaron survive in Seattle.
Jacklyn ran a non-for-profit foundation that
provided the
Seattle area with volunteer workers (The Jonathan
Charity). She later gave up the foundation to be a
homemaker in 2000. However, she remained on
the board of directors until her death.
She was preceded in death by her father, Jerry Lee
Krause in 1995, and her mother, Anna Jo (Bechard)
Krause in 2002.
Other survivors also include her sister Christie Jo
(Krause) Flint of Seattle, WA and her Aunt Kathrine
Rose (Kay) Bechard of Chicago, IL.
Visitation will be Friday from 4-7 at Willow Springs
Funeral Home in Seattle, WA.
Funeral will be Saturday, August 3rd at 11:00am at
St. Mark's Catholic Church on 8th St. Seattle, Wa.

Chapter 1

The Spelling Bee

"Eidetic." This would be a hard word for any eleven-year-old to spell, but not Aaron Casey. As he stands at the microphone, the judges and audience await his answer to what could be his final word at the National Spelling Bee in Seattle, Washington. Now, Aaron knows this word very well because it was applied to him many years before he could even spell it. Just to make sure he is hearing the word correctly, and like any spelling bee participant, Aaron asks for the judge to repeat the word and read the definition. The judge replies, "I-'de-tik, marked by or involving extraordinarily accurate and vivid recall especially of visual images." Without hesitation Aaron spells the word correctly and sits back down.

While sitting there patiently awaiting his final opponent's answer to the next word, he thinks of when he first saw the word, eidetic. Aaron's psychologist, Dr. Blake, labeled him with an eidetic memory or photographic memory at the age of four. One of Dr. Blake's first obstacles for Aaron was reconstructing an in-progress game of chess after only one minute of studying the arrangement of the pieces. Even though, at the age of four, this was Aaron's first time seeing a chess set. He reconstructed the game flawlessly. Assuming that this was a coincidence, Dr. Blake tried the same exercise, only he blindfolded Aaron before he reconstructed the game. To Dr. Blake's surprise, the blindfold actually seemed to make the exercise easier for Aaron, other than having to feel the pieces before he placed them on the board. Following a few more tests, Aaron was definitely one of the brightest children Dr. Blake had worked with, and he helped Aaron to develop his gift over the years. Spelling is one of the many things Dr. Blake has pushed Aaron to succeed at, knowing that he would do well especially in a competition setting.

One of the main reasons that Aaron began seeing Dr. Blake was a very traumatic experience that he encountered as a toddler. His mother was killed when he was only 2 ½ years old, and he was present in the same room. This changed Aaron's life forever, mainly because his father was convicted of the murder. His father, Mel Casey, has pleaded innocent from the beginning.

Since then, Aaron has lived with his Aunt Christie Flint and Uncle Greg Flint in Seattle. Christie is the younger sister of Aaron's mother, Jacklyn Casey. Christie and Greg were married one year before Jackie's death, and Aaron moved in at a time when Christie and Greg were just about ready to start their own family. They both love Aaron as their own and neither one seemed to think twice about how it would have been if this had never happened.

Aaron's father is serving his time at a prison not far from Seattle and Aaron visits him frequently. Aaron believes his father is innocent, and so does his Aunt Christie and Uncle Greg. After his spelling bee Christie is supposed to take Aaron to see his father, but Aaron is taking a little longer to win this year and it is getting too late to make visiting hours. After a few more words, Aaron does go on to win his third national championship in a row.

Aaron and Christie see Dr. Blake walking toward them in the crowded halls of the Auditorium. As Dr. Blake gets close enough, he says, "Good job Aaron, I knew you could do it for a third time!" Christie agreed and said, "Yeah Aaron, we all told you if you try hard enough you can do anything." Aaron didn't care about the trophy or the complements. His dad was on his mind at the moment. Aaron says with hope, "Do we still have enough time to go see Dad?" Christie replies, "I'm not sure, it depends on traffic." Dr. Blake jumps in and says, "How about I take you out for ice cream to celebrate Aaron?" Before Aaron even has a chance to answer, Christie says, "We really need to get going either way; it has been a long day." Dr. Blake agrees and says, "Yeah, I will have to take a rain check. I do have to get back to the office. Congratulations Aaron, I will see you tomorrow. Don't forget your journal." Then Dr. Blake realizes what he just said and must laugh. He tells Aaron, "Never mind, just be on time." Aaron nods his head with a smile and says, "Thanks Dr. Blake, I'll see you tomorrow." "Bye Dr. Blake, thank you for coming." Christie said as Dr. Blake walked towards the exit. Christie looks to Aaron and says, "Ok, are you ready?' Aaron replies, "Yeah, I take it we are not going to see Dad?" Christie answers, "We should really try to get home, it is getting late, and I need to get supper started before Greg gets home, OK?" Aaron agrees and they head back to the car.

As they head home Aaron is still thinking about his Dad, and how he has always felt so strongly about his father not being the person that killed his Mom. He wishes that he could remember more from that day. Dr. Blake said that he could help him to remember that day, but Aaron has always tried not to talk about it with Dr. Blake. It is something that Aaron blocks out, and he is always worried that he will remember his father committing the brutal crime. Since Aaron was only

2 years old it is a little easier for him to block it out than if he were older, but he does have periodic dreams about that day. Someday, maybe, he will muster up enough courage to take Dr. Blake up on his offer, but not anytime soon.

Aaron looks over and asks, "Aunt Christie, you still think my dad is innocent, right?" Without hesitation she answers, "Of course. Why do you ask?" Aaron looks out the window and replies, "I dunno, I was just wondering if you had any doubts." Christie thinks for a second and replies, "Well, I can remember the way he would look at your mother, and there is just no way he would have done it. They had too much love for one another. Has Dr. Blake been bringing it up?" Aaron answers, "Well, yeah. Over the past couple weeks he has brought it up. He said he has an old college roommate that does phenomenal things with kids and their memories. He wanted to reach out to him after he talked to you of course." Christie with a stern voice says, "Are you ok with this Aaron?" Aaron says, "I guess so, I just hope Dad is not the one I always dream about from that day." Christie replies, "Well, that was a long time ago, and I will let you decide on your own as to whether or not you should continue with this new therapy technique with Dr. Blake. Just don't let Dr. Blake pressure you into it, because I know how he can push you sometimes." Aaron says, "This is one thing he will not push me on, but I do want to help Dad."

Chapter 2

The Chopper

Well, they make it back to the Flint household, a two-story suburban home in a typical suburban neighborhood. It's the same house that Jacklyn was murdered in. Mel insisted that they move in since they were taking care of Aaron, who at the time was so young. Greg and Christie were living in a trailer at the time. They were saving for their dream home when their whole lives changed.

Christie and Aaron pull in and open the garage to find Greg working on his motorcycle that has been chopped into a thousand pieces over the past three years. Someday, Greg plans to take Christie for a trip along the coast all the way to Baja. He has only had it running three times in the past three years though and then he buys something or adds something to the bike that requires major changes. Christie parks in the driveway and they head into the house through the garage. Greg sees them and says, "Hey Slugger, looks like you won again? That trophy is smaller than last year. Did you still get 1st or did an underdog take you out?" Aaron smiles and says, "Heck yeah I won again, but the trophy budget must have been cut back." Greg laughs and then says "Well at least you have that over with. Now you can practice with the team this week for our big game Thursday against the Redbirds."

Greg coaches Aaron's little league baseball team. Aaron isn't the best athlete, but he has fun and Greg likes to see him participate in sports. As Greg looks for his socket wrench, he says, "You know those Redbirds are undefeated this year, so far; but we can handle them, right Slugger?" Christie interrupts, "I'm gonna go start dinner." Greg says, "OK babe, I will be finished here soon. Just let me clean up."

Chapter 3

Detective Roberts Visit

Dr. Blake pulls into his office parking lot about 15 minutes late this morning. He walks into the waiting room of his doctor's office only expecting to see Mrs. Kawley at the front desk with his usual cup of coffee waiting. He was so late this morning that he had decided to wear his tie and belt that he keeps in the office for emergencies only. Mrs. Kawley usually opens the office at 8:30am and their first appointment is not until 9:30. So normally the waiting room is empty when they greet each other in the mornings; however, when Dr. Blake walks in he sees a man standing at the front sliding window with a black jacket that says DETECTIVE across the back in yellow print. He looks at Mrs. Kawley stunned and looks over at the Detective as he walks up and asks, "Is everything OK Detective?" Mrs. Kawley just smiles while the man responds, "Hi, I am Detective Jon Roberts with the Seattle Police Department, and I have some questions for you on a case I am working on." Mrs. Kawley jumps in and says, "Yes he was just showing me the file he has on Aaron." Dr. Blake's eyes got big, and he questioned the detective, "Aaron?" Detective Roberts said, "Yes Aaron Casey, he has been a patient of yours for quite a while, am I correct?" Dr. Blake says, "Yes, he has. Let's take this back to my office where it is more private."

Dr. Blake walks back to his office and Det. Roberts follows him. Dr. Blake goes straight to his closet and takes out a tie and a belt that will match his shirt and shoes respectively. Det. Roberts starts off by saying, "This is a nice office you have here. How long have you been in practice?" Dr. Blake pretends like he didn't hear the question and replies, "You said you are here for Aaron?" Det. Roberts replies, "Yes, are you allowed to talk about Aaron and his visits at all?" Dr. Blake says, "No I am not. Considering, first he is a minor, and second it is against my oath as a therapist. All patient sessions are totally confidential under the therapist/client confidentiality clause I have everyone sign before we begin working together." Det. Roberts decides to ease into the questioning then, "Can I ask non patient related questions then?" Dr. Blake says, "Sure, go ahead." Det. Roberts asks, "Do you keep individual files on all your patients, and are they under lock and key?" Dr. Blake answers, "Yes and yes" Det. Roberts continues, "Do you keep paper files, electronic files, or both?" Dr. Blake says, "Well I started with paper only and in 2006 we transitioned to electronic filing." Det. Roberts decides to ask about Aaron here anyway, "During your time with

Aaron has he ever discussed any details of his mother's death." Dr. Blake asks, "Didn't you hear me earlier? We will need permission to talk about Aaron's time here from his guardian and from Aaron himself." Det. Roberts seems disgusted with this response but continues, "Well I can tell you we have some rather new developments in his father's case, and we may eventually need that permission granted. We may also need to speak with Aaron himself soon. I wanted to drop by today and give you a heads up on a call we will be making here tomorrow from the District Attorney's office. The new DA, Bryce Edwards, has some items he would like to discuss with you, and we heard you have a special bond with Aaron so before going to his Aunt and Uncle, the legal guardians, we thought you may be of some help with information before we jump right into the reinvestigation of the case. Who should I contact at the Flint residence? Is it Greg Flint or Christie?" Dr. Blake quickly answers, "Christie is who I usually deal with. Greg works long hours." Detective Roberts says, "OK well I will leave you to your day. We will call the office later today to confirm a time for that call tomorrow." Dr. Blake says, "OK I will have Mrs. Kawley open a slot of time tomorrow for a call. Have a good day Detective."

Chapter 4

The Conference Call

Mrs. Kawley hangs up the phone after taking an appointment and suddenly the phone rings again just as she puts down the receiver. She answers, "Hello you have reached the office of Dr. Thomas Blake. How may I help you." Detective Roberts responds, "Hi Mrs. Kawley this is Detective Roberts from the Seattle Police Department. I am here with District Attorney Bryce Edwards. We are ready for that 2pm conference call we have scheduled." Mrs. Kawley answers, "Oh yes, he is ready and waiting for your call in his office. Let me transfer you. Please hold the line." She pushes the transfer button and dials Dr. Blake's office number. "Blake here." Mrs. Kawley says, "Dr. Blake I have your 2pm conference call waiting, when I hang up they will be on the other line."

Dr. Blake hears the connection change, and he answers, "Hello this is Dr. Blake." He pushes the speakerphone button, hangs up the handset, and stands up from his desk. "Dr. Blake, this is Bryce Edwards, and I have with me Detective Jon Roberts. He was at your office yesterday." Det. Roberts jumps in and says, "Hello Dr. Blake." Dr. Blake says, "Hello gentlemen, how can I be of service." The DA continues, "Dr. Blake, we have an

14

interesting situation brewing here at Seattle PD that includes my predecessor, Ben Henke. What I am about to tell you is strictly confidential and cannot be disclosed to anyone until we have all the pieces in place. Can we trust you to keep this investigation to yourself and not let it leave your office?" Dr. Blake agrees and asks, "How can I help with this?" The DA continues, "We have uncovered some trial manipulation, and some plea deals that were falsified. We are looking to break these cases open and have decided to start with the Melvin Casey trial. We received an anonymous tip that some of the inmates were given plea deals that included information to lead into some of the convictions. In return, the inmates that cooperated were given a reduced sentence. Inmates would get less time if they lied about being involved. The previous DA would tell them what to say in court and then if it helped the case they would get a shorter sentence. We believe that Melvin was somehow involved since he was the defense lawyer for many of these inmates and in some of the trials. We also believe that Melvin Casey may have uncovered this "rat's nest" and was very close to exposing the individuals involved. It is possible that he was framed for his wife's murder, and he was silenced with the threat of harm to Aaron while he served his time. This is why we are starting with his case."

Dr. Blake stops pacing and looks at the phone. Dr. Blake says, "I guess I need to ask again; how can I help?" The DA answers, "I need your help with Aaron. We have heard he has a good memory. We would like you to see how far back he can remember." Dr. Blake jumps in, "Guys, I am not sure I feel comfortable on this one." Det. Roberts jumps in on the conversation and says, "Dr. Blake, is there anyone out there you would recommend for this type of interrogation?" Dr. Blake thinks and says, "Yes, I have an old college roommate that has worked in this realm for many years. He specializes with young children too. His name is Dr. Brian Jaims out of San Francisco. I can give him a call and see if he can work with Aaron. I have a feeling this would work better if Dr. Jaims was to work with Aaron here in my office since he is comfortable with this setting." The DA responds, "That would be great. Can you give him a call and get back to us today?" Dr. Blake agrees and tells them he will call him right now.

Dr. Blake says goodbye and gives a call to Mrs. Kawley. "Candace, will you look up Dr. Brian Jaims office number and get him on the line for me. I must talk to him right away. Mrs. Kawley answers, "Sure I can get him on the line as soon as possible."

Dr. Blake walks back to the break room and grabs a bottle of water from the fridge. He walks back to his office and his phone is already ringing. He answers and it is Mrs. Kawley with Dr. Jaims on the line. Dr. Blake begins, "Hey Brian, it's been a few years. How is it going?" Dr. Jaims replies, "It's going great Thom. What's happening up in Seattle these days?" Dr. Blake answers, "Well I wondered if you remember a client of mine, Aaron Casey. I have worked with him for the last 8 or 9 years. You met him when he was about 3 or 4 years old. This was when I first started working with him and I had you do that eidetic memory evaluation. Do you remember anything about Aaron?" Dr. Jaims laughs and replies, "How could I forget Aaron? The kid was brilliant. He must be 11 or 12 now. What is he up to these days? Did he take over your practice yet? Ha. Ha." Dr. Blake says, "Not exactly. I am still working with him on a weekly basis, and he is incredible. However, we have come to a hurdle here and I was wondering if I could get some assistance." Dr. Jaims says, "Sure, how can I help?" Dr. Blake answers, "Well we have to go back into his early memories to extract some information about his parents." Dr. Jaims jumps in, "Oh yeah, his mother had just died a year or so before I saw him and his father was on trial if I remember correctly." Dr. Blake responded, "Yes, you are correct." Dr. Jaims asks, "What ever happened with that?" Dr. Blake answers, "His father was convicted and has been serving time since Aaron was 4." Dr. Jaims says, "I am sorry to hear that. How has Aaron been holding up since?" Dr. Blake answers, "He has been living with his Aunt and Uncle since then and he comes to see me on Wednesdays and Saturdays. I just got off the phone with the new district attorney and the Seattle Police Department. They are looking into a retrial for his father. They would like to see if Aaron can remember anything from that day his mother died. If you can remember, he was at the house with her when she was killed. I know this is a big ask but do you think you can help with some treatments to help spark his memory from his toddler years?" Dr. Jaims answers, "Well I have a client that has a deposition scheduled for tomorrow but after that I am free for a little while. Can it wait until early next week? I can possibly help on Sundays, Mondays and Tuesdays. My office is closed on those days. I actually just finished a case that brought back some memories of a 17-year-old. His father and mother died when he was 3 and he could not remember the years he had with them. We were able to restore his memory of up to 8 major life events. We found his Aunt that moved to Canada and she had photos and some items that brought his memories back. I would like to use some of the techniques that I used with him. I found that photo elicitation along with some hypnotherapy works wonders." Dr. Blake jumps in, "Can I have Mrs. Kawley call your office to set up some dates?" Dr. Jaims replies, "Candace still works for you?" Dr. Blake says, "Yes she is my rock." Dr. Jaims continues, "Sure that will work. I will get some packages ready and send them over to your office. I will have Janet, my new assistant, coordinate that with Mrs. Kawley. I also think it would be a good jump start if you go see Melvin Casey in Prison. We need to get some information from him. I will come up with some ideas you can take with you to ask him about. This will mostly be Aaron's major life events from when they were together as a family. Birthdays, holidays, trips, family get-togethers that they may have shared. I will also ask you to plan a walk for Aaron in your next session. I will send some photos in the package with some strict directions for you to follow in a blue folder. I do this with some of my new patients and when I make my first visit to your office next week, we will revisit the walk to see what he remembers. After you get the packages, if you have questions, you can call me. Let me give you my personal cell just in case you can't reach me at the office. 454-555-0987."

Dr. Blake ends the conversation and wonders just how much work this is going to be. He also wonders if it is something he will want to put Aaron through. Aaron has never really wanted to dig that deep into the past with his parents. Maybe he is old enough that he will be ready to remember, but it is not likely. We will have to see.

Dr. Blake dials the phone and gets Mrs. Kawley to answer. Mrs. Kawley says, "Yes Dr. Blake?" "Candace, can you get me the DA back on the phone so I can update him on Dr. Jaims?" Mrs. Kawley answers, "Yes give me a second to get Margie all settled here. She is your 3:30 appointment, by the way." He looks at his clock and it is sitting at 3:05 pm. Dr. Blake says, "OK, she is a bit early so I will see her after I talk with the DA. This shouldn't take long."

Dr. Blake hangs up the hand set and gives a sigh. He thinks to himself, *"Boy what a day this has been."* Then his phone rang. Dr. Blake picks up and says, "Bryce, is that you?" Bryce answers back, "Hi Dr. Blake, any news on your college buddy?" Dr. Blake answers, "Yes, he is on board. He is putting a package together as we speak to work on getting Aaron on the track to get us some answers from the past. He will be here on Sunday, Monday, and Tuesday to begin working with Aaron. When Aaron is here on Wednesday we will begin training. Would you like to call Christie Flint before we begin, or would you like me to break the news?" The DA answers, "Hey, it would be a good idea if she first hears it from you and we can follow up later when she is already knee deep in the fire. Maybe we can keep it as just a new therapy you are trying with Dr. Jaims and see where it goes. Maybe Dr. Jaims will find out that Aaron will not produce anything we can use so let's just see how the first 3 days go." Dr. Blake said, "That is fine with me and if she asks for anything deeper, I will not be able to hold back. I will be forced to tell her what is going on. I will not lie to her about it." The DA agrees and they both hang up and go on with finishing their days.

Chapter 5

The Groundbreaking Study

Sunday mornings are Aaron's favorites. He goes to see his father, Mel. Greg yells into Aaron's bedroom, "Aaron....time to get up Champ! We've got some work to do on the bike." Christie says, "What? You're going to work on the chopper again this morning?" Greg says, "Yeah Babe....gotta finish what I started last night. It's almost done." Christie laughs and says, "Yeah right....That will be the day." Greg quickly replies, "Whatever....come on Aaron, let's go. Oh yeah babe, Dr. Blake called this morning and asked for you. He said it was important for Aaron's next visit."

While they are outside Christie decides to call Dr. Blake to find out his plan for Aaron this week. "Guys, don't be long out there we'll be leaving in about an hour to visit your dad." As Christie sees them out the door to the garage, she goes straight to the phone to call Dr. Blake. This will be the perfect opportunity to chat with him since Aaron is out helping Greg. Being that it's a Sunday she tries his cell phone first. "Thomas Blake here." Out of breath Dr. Blake answers his cell phone that was clipped to his belt. "Hi Dr. Blake, its Christie Flint, have I called at a bad time?" "No, I'm down here at the office rearranging a bit." Dr.

Blake adds, while still trying to catch his breath. What can I do for you this beautiful Sunday morning?" Christie says, "Well I got your message, and you have me wondering about what you will be doing with Aaron this week? You never called about an upcoming appointment." Dr. Blake answers, "Well to be honest with you Christie, it's a new technique one of my old college roommates has introduced to some of his clients & he suggested that I try it with Aaron. It will eventually include a hypnotism technique that will take us further than we ever have with Aaron and understanding what he remembers from the past and how it will affect him in the future." Christie jumps in, "Why haven't you told me about this until now? Is it dangerous?" Dr. Blake answers, "No, not at all.....I was going to give you the details at Aaron's next appointment. It's going to take some time before we can begin the sessions, anyhow. There is some strict preparation beforehand." "Like what?" exclaims Christie. "Well, I can give you the details Wednesday but from what I have seen this morning in the packages I received from Dr. Jaims, it does involve some herbs and at least 10 hours of sleep every night for the 2 weeks prior. The serotonin levels and hormone levels must be perfect for it to work. I would like to do a baseline test with him Wednesday if you all agree to pursue this groundbreaking study. Christie jumps in again, "Groundbreaking study?" Dr. Blake explains, "Yes, my college classmate, Dr. Brian Jaims will be involved, and he will document all activities as we practice this technique, I will give you all of the paperwork Wednesday along with Dr. Jaims' resume and references so you can check up on him, if you would like." Christie asks, "OK, so what is the timeline and schedule for this, quote, groundbreaking study?" Blake sheepishly adds, "Well, I was going to give you all a week to think it over then we would start as soon as possible considering the 2-week prep. Then it would be three times a week for about a month, probably, nine to twelve sessions." Christie checks the clock on the stove in the kitchen and says, "Alright we'll talk about this more Wednesday." Blake says, "I'll have the prospectus ready for you then. Dr. Jaims' firm is fully funding the study, including the herbs and meal rebates along with some minor patient compensation." Christie says, "OK, Dr. Blake....I'll talk it over with Greg and Aaron tonight and we'll decide Wednesday. Goodbye."

Chapter 6

The Stroll

Wednesday arrives and Christie and Aaron, like usual, are 10 minutes early for the last appointment of the day at Dr. Blake's office. Aaron has his journal, and Christie has on her best face for Mrs. Kawley but she is not ready to deal with Dr. Blake and his "new therapy" with Aaron.

Mrs. Kawley says, "You can go back now." and Christie leads the way. She goes to Dr. Blake's office, and tells Aaron to go wait in the break room. Aaron agrees and she walks into Dr. Blake's office and closes the door. She asks him point blank, "What is this all about Dr. Blake? You need to explain yourself here." Dr. Blake takes off his glasses and sits back in his chair. Dr. Blake looks her in the eyes and says, "How are you this afternoon, Christie?" She replies, "I am fine, but I want to know what is going on here and I want to know now!" Dr. Blake smiles and says, "Well I have an old college roommate that has been doing some amazing things with very gifted children around Aaron's age. Some of them are really excelling with their abilities. I ran across his website and have been thinking of calling him to see if he would have some ideas for Aaron. I definitely wanted to talk with you and Greg first before we dive right into it. Now one thing I want to warn you about with this technique is that it does stimulate the older memory banks. Aaron may be led into a better comprehension of what happened with Jackie and Mel. That is where the technique begins with photo elicitation therapy. Once you break the walls of long-term memory the sky's the limit for both short term and long term memory." Christie thinks for a second and then says, "So you're telling me there is a risk of him remembering exactly what happened that day?" Dr. Blake presses his lips and then says, "Yes unfortunately there is a good chance we could pass through his memories of that day. I can call Dr. Jaims tonight and get some more information so that we can begin this therapy right away if you are OK with it. We really need to get Aaron to the next level." Christie says, "Okay well I would really like to see how Aaron feels about all of this? Is there any way we can bring him in and talk to him about it." Dr. Blake answers, "Well, I'm not sure if that's a great idea today. I'm going to take a walk with him, and we'll see how he feels about it. If you don't mind, I would like to ask him myself." Christie thinks for a moment and then she says, "Okay that's fine. He trusts you the most and tonight I will talk to Greg about it." Dr. Blake says, "Okay let me go get Aaron and we will start today's therapy."

Dr. Blake walks back to the break room, and he sees Aaron doodling in his journal. Aaron looks up and says, "Hey! Dr. Blake how's it going?" Dr. Blake says, "Hey, it's going pretty good Aaron. Today, I have something fun planned. We're going to do a little walk in the building across the street. I would like to show you some pictures they have on display over there. If you're okay with that?" Aaron closes his notebook, and he says, "Yeah that sounds like a good idea." Dr. Blake continues, "Let's go say goodbye to Christie and we will head out." They both walk back to the office where Christie is waiting, and she greets them at the door. She says, "Okay Aaron, I must go run some errands. I will be back in about an hour." Aaron smiles and tells her, "Okay, see you in a little bit." Dr. Blake looks at Aaron and says, "Hey let me grab my coat and then we can head out."

Dr. Blake grabbed his coat, and they walked out towards the front. When they get to the front Dr. Blake tells Mrs. Kawley, "We'll be back in a little bit, we're going to go for a walk." Mrs. Kawley says, "Okay see you guys soon."

Once Dr. Blake and Aaron get across the street, they enter a building that is about the same size as Dr. Blake's office. This building has three stories, it's made of brick, and there are tall windows to look outside.   Aaron says, "I've never been in this building, but I've seen it every time I come to see you. It looks pretty neat inside." Dr. Blake answers, "Yes, this building has been here longer than the one I'm in. There is a local Museum up on the third floor and the second floor is mostly office space. The first floor, as you can see, is just open and there's a large lobby. This is where I would like to take our walk today." At this point, Aaron sees Dr. Blake reach into his pocket, he pulls out his cellphone and pushes a button and he says, "Okay, let's go. There are some cool pictures I have seen here on lunch the past couple weeks that I want to show you."

As they walk into the main lobby, they start to the right and work the lobby in a counterclockwise direction. Dr. Blake shows him a few pictures and he walks through the hallways along the circular path. In most of the photos Dr. Blake stops and comments on the photo but keeps walking. When they get to the end, they walk out of the back door. This opens to the alleyway behind the building. They turn the corner and head back towards Dr. Blake's office. Dr. Blake points out a wall mural displaying an ad for a local auto repair shop. Dr. Blake pulls out a camera and says, "I always liked this mural, and I would like to take a picture of it for my office." He steps to the back side of the alley and aims his camera. He says, "I love the old Chevy Belair from the 50's. All the chrome and the old gas station pumps just look neat." Aaron agrees and says, "That it is pretty neat." Then Aaron hears a loud pop and they both start to smell something strange almost like burnt rubber. They both cough and hold their noses. Dr. Blake says, "Okay, let's get back to the office."

When they go back to Dr. Blake's office, Mrs. Kawley is waiting there. She tells Dr. Blake that she has to leave early if he could lock up that would be great. Dr. Blake said, "That's fine, have a nice evening. We'll see you tomorrow. I can lock up."

Dr. Blake and Aaron head back to his office. They take off their coats and sit down. Aaron says to Dr. Blake, "You know a lot about those pictures in that building. Have you been there before? Dr. Blake says, "Yes, every once in a while, I stop there on my lunch break." Dr. Blake sits in his chair and decides to tell Aaron the next step for his therapy. Dr. Blake begins, "Aaron it seems to me that we have hit a wall with your progress. I have a friend in San Francisco that also does therapy with gifted children. I am not sure if you remember him but when you were four, he came and did an evaluation. His name is Dr. Brian Jaims. Do you remember him at all?" Aaron says, "Yes, I do remember him. He is the one with the colored cups and the photographs, right?" Dr. Blake agrees and says, "Yes, I would like to work with him more if you don't mind. He has been part of a huge breakthrough on the mind using photographs linked to memories. His technique is called photo elicitation therapy or P.E.T. The way he works is to start from the beginning of your memory banks. This is where I am hesitant with you. I want to know if you're okay with going back to your toddler years?" Aaron gives a frown and a shoulder shrug. He says, "I am not sure I can remember that far back. I have tried to remember my mom before she died, and it is hard for me. We have discussed that before, and it still seems that I just can't remember that far back. Most of my memories start when I began living with Christie and Greg." Dr. Blake chimes in, "Well, this is where Dr. Jaims is an expert. He will use some techniques to break through those walls we have come to find recently. Once we are through those walls, it will open up your memory to become stronger. Your short-term memory and long-term memory will improve dramatically. He has proven that once you open those early memory banks the sky's the limit." Aaron looks up from his hands to Dr. Blake and says, "I think I'm ready for this." Dr. Blake continues, "The techniques that Dr. Jaims uses can be a steppingstone as a way to learn how to manipulate your memory banks." Aaron says, "I should be fine with this and as long as Christie and Greg are okay with it, I will continue with this therapy Dr. Jaims is proposing."

At this point, they hear a knock at the door. Dr. Blake says, "Come in." The door opens to reveal Christie. She looks at Aaron and says, "Are you ready?" Aaron says, "Yes I am ready. Did you know that Dr. Jaims is coming back? Christie says, "Yes, you know of him already?" Aaron answers, "Yes, I remember him from when I was 4." Christie looks to Dr. Blake and says, "That's the same guy?" Dr. Blake agrees and says, "I will drop off a package at your house tomorrow, so we can begin treatment. When will you be free?" Christie thinks for a second and says, "Why don't you swing by in the morning when Aaron heads off for school?" Aaron looks at Dr. Blake and says, "That would be at 8 a.m." Dr. Blake agrees and he decides to walk them to the door so he can lock up.

Chapter 7

The Package

Dr. Blake arrives at the Flint household he pushes the button to open the hatch to his Explorer. He walks around to the back of his SUV and pulls out a large box. He closes the hatch and begins to walk to the front door of the Flint household. He rings the doorbell. Christie answers the door, and she says, "Oh. Hi Dr. Blake, come on in. You can put that box over on the table and come on in for a cup of coffee." Dr. Blake sets down the box and walks back to the kitchen with Christie. When he gets to the kitchen, Aaron is sitting down eating a bowl of cereal. He is all ready for school. Dr. Blake says, "Hey Aaron, how are you doing this morning." Aaron replies, "I'm doing pretty good. I am running a little late though." Then all of the sudden the doorbell rang, Aaron got up and ran to the door, he knew it is probably his friend, Miley. When he got to the door, he opened it up and he was right. "Good morning, Miley," Aaron says. Miley says, "Are you ready, or what?" Aaron says, "Yeah let me grab my book bag and then we can go." Aaron runs back to the kitchen and looks under the table where his book bag is on the ground. He picks it up and says, "Hey Dr. Blake, we'll see you later. I'm heading to school." Christie says, "Hey good luck on that math test today and be careful going to school. Have a good day!"

Aaron and Miley head out to the sidewalk and start to walk to school. Miley says to Aaron, "What's Dr. Blake doing at your house this morning?" Aaron tells her about the new therapy treatments Dr. Blake and Dr. Jaims will be doing over the next few weeks. Miley says, "Won't you be scared to know what happened, when your mom died?" Aaron says, "I don't think I remember anyway so I'm not too worried about it."

Back at the house Dr. Blake grabs the box from the table and takes it into the kitchen. Once he gets to the kitchen, he opens it up and pulls out a folder. Dr. Blake says, "Now Christie, in this folder is all the instructions. I'm going to go through it all with you now and you can keep it to make sure you stay on track. Now like I told you before, Dr. Jaims office works under a grant from the State of California. So, all these materials are paid for through the grant. In turn, this means they must log everything they do with Aaron. Aaron will be assigned a number, and it is totally confidential. The logs are kept by the State of California and the files will not be used for anything other than training purposes. These logs can be seen by licensed and registered psychiatrists in the State of California only. Currently the only professor that is allowed to use these for teaching purposes is Dr. Nathan David at the University of California at Berkeley. Like I said, it is strictly confidential, and each participant is assigned a number only. Their names are not revealed. So, let's begin by looking in the folder as these items have very strict directions that need to be followed to the best of your ability. Before we go any further, do you have any questions?" She answers, "Yes. Do you want any of this coffee or not?" Dr. Blake laughs and says, "Sure." Christie says, "Let's go to the table and talk about this."

Dr. Blake grabs the box and moves it over to the table. He pulls out a box that is full of flashcards. He opens the box and pulls out the flash cards to show Christie. Dr. Blake says, "Now these are the photos that Aaron has to study 20 minutes before bed." He reaches into the box and pulls out a CD. He tells her, "This is the CD that is to be played with the photos. The photos are all numbered 1 to 48. He will need to see them in order. Do you have a CD player in the kitchen?" Christie says, "Yes, over by the fridge on the counter." Dr. Blake walks over and puts the disc into the CD player and pushes play. He sees the remote control to the CD player and grabs it. He walks back to the table and pulls out the flash cards. He holds them in a way that they can both see the photographs. The CD player projects a voice that says, "Let's begin. After the beep, please move to the next photo in order. Please look at photo number one." Then a voice says, "Pickle," and the CD player makes a beep sound. Christie says, "Now pause the player. I don't understand what the picture represents in regard to a pickle. This is a photo of a meadow. Am I correct?" Dr. Blake says, "Yes. Sometimes there will not be a connection, it is only a word that will need to be recalled later. It is for memory purposes only. In this case, the Meadow is green in color, which is a small connection to a green pickle. Some people make a connection to a memory based on eyesight, hearing, feeling, or touch. Have you ever heard a song on the radio, and it takes you back to a special time in your life?" Christie answers, "Well yes I have." Dr. Blake says, "This is how it works. Some of these photos will show us how much Aaron will use his eyesight for memory and how much will be used by his imagination of a certain situation." Christie says, "Okay, I have seen enough. What else do you have in the Box?"

Dr. Blake puts the cards back in the box and walks over to grab the CD from the player. He puts those items back in the box and pulls out some containers that hold pills. Dr. Blake says, "These are the herbs that Aaron will have to take daily. They are all natural and combined with the Sleep regimen they will work together to help his concentration. Over 200 patients in California have used these methods and there were only minor side effects. Most of them had an upset stomach in the beginning until the stomach got used to the substance."

Dr. Blake continues, "Now let's go over the sleeping regimen. Aaron will have to achieve 10 hours of sleep by Sunday this weekend. We start the next two nights at 8 and a half hours. Then on Thursday and Friday we will move to 9 hours and Saturday will be 9 and 1/2 hours. So, by Sunday night he can achieve 10 hours of sleep. Then we will need him to get 10 hours of sleep until we are finished with the therapy. How many hours does he sleep now?" Christie answers, "About 9 hours so we should be okay." Dr. Blake now asks, "Christie, is there any way we can get some photos of Aaron in a few major events from when Jackie was still alive?" Christie says, "Wait here there are two albums upstairs that Jackie had before she died you can take those." Dr. Blake says, "Perfect, thank you we will be using these for testing purposes."

When Christie comes back with the photo albums Dr. Blake says, "Christie if you have any questions, you know my number and in the folder is Dr. Jaims card. He will be here Sunday, Monday, and Tuesday next week for Aaron's first tests. Mrs. Kawley will call you to set up some times for those days. Please make sure to follow that information closely in that blue folder in the box. It is very important." Christie says, "OK, we will. Thanks for your time on this. Make sure you also thank Dr. Jaims for us. I hope it will get Aaron to a better place with his past. It is the whole reason we have brought him to you in the last 8 years." Dr. Blake says, "OK I will get back to the office. I have an appointment in 20 minutes that I would rather not be late for. Thanks for your time today, Christie. Goodbye."

Chapter 8

The Prisoner

Mel Casey paced back and forth along the south wall of his jail cell when the guard approached and said, "Melvin Casey......You have a visitor!" Mel poked out his hands to be cuffed so fast it was like he had been waiting for that news all week. Once he was cuffed his cell door slid open and the guard walked him across the building to a private visitor's cell. They sat him at a table across from a man he had never seen before. Slender bodied man, with dark hair and glasses. Dressed well; collared shirt and tie, but no suit jacket so Mel figured it wasn't just another lawyer. Mel spoke up first, "Do I know you?" Then a light bulb flashed in Mel's brain. "Wait, let me guess. You're Dr. Blake?" The man said, "Yes, I'm Dr. Blake. I'm here to talk to you about your son, Aaron." This is the first time Mel had met Dr. Blake, but he had heard enough about him from Aaron's visits.

Dr. Blake cleared his throat and started, "I am about to begin a new therapy technique with Aaron called photo elicitation therapy or P.E.T. It could possibly spark some memories of his years as an infant and toddler. I would like to know more about the time you spent with Aaron before your conviction if that's OK with you?" Melvin hesitated,

"I guess that would be fine. Gets me out of my jail cell for a while."

Dr. Blake reaches into his leather briefcase and pulls out a notebook and a voice recorder. Suddenly Mel makes a puzzled frown, as Dr. Blake pushes the record button and sets down the voice recorder. Dr. Blake begins, "Now Mel...It's OK if I call you Mel, right?" Mel shakes his head in agreement. "Mel, I'll need your permission to record our conversation today. I have talked with the Seattle Police Department and any findings in our therapies with your son, Aaron Casey, could possibly be used in court sometime in the future. If you have any objection to the subject of any questions I ask, you can just say "pass" and we can move on to something else. Do I have your permission to record?" Mel was a lawyer before he was put in jail so like usual, he thinks, maybe I should talk with my lawyer about this? Before Mel can answer, Dr. Blake jumps in, "Mel, I have also spoken with your lawyer, and he said this new therapy probably wouldn't hold up in court and he is fine with it if you are. He also reviewed my questions via email and has approved the questions." Mel thought about it and agreed to answer the questions.

Dr. Blake begins, "OK Mel, I need you to think of 5 major events or tragic events that happened around Aaron." Mel looked up at the ceiling of the visiting cell and said, "Boy, this will be a hard one." This is when Dr. Blake reached into his briefcase again and pulled out the photo albums he received from Christie. Dr. Blake said, "Well think of special occasions, like birthdays or vacations. Were there any moments you can remember that Aaron was a part of celebrating?" He answered quickly, "Yes there was. Aaron had a birthday party. It was a Barney theme. Man, I hated that big purple dinosaur, but Aaron loved it. His mother loved it too because it kept his attention most of the time." Dr. Blake says, "I think I have some photos here from that day." He flips through a few pages and finds the birthday party with Barney. Dr. Blake asks, "Well was there anything at the party you remember, specifically." Mel answered, "Yes, I remember that Jackie's mom held on to Aaron most of the day. She loved him and spoiled the damn kid whenever she visited Boston. She came for a week, and it was the day after she arrived, so Aaron was fresh in her hands during the beginning of the trip. Even when we sang happy birthday to the kid he was on her lap, and she helped blow out his candles. My brother even came dressed as a clown and he was a huge hit. He made balloon animals and juggled. He didn't have any white paint, so he used yellow on his face, and it was a little spooky for some of the kiddos. Toward the end of the party, I ended up pushing him in the pool and it was hilarious. All the kids loved it." Dr. Blake said, "OK great, I see a lot of pictures here that will help us with Aaron remembering that day. Any other events you remember? "Yes." Mel answered. "We took a trip to Boston for Aaron's baptism. He was baptized in the same Catholic Church I was baptized in. And Father Gerald was still alive to do the services. He was on his last leg, and he had an eye patch because the glaucoma had clouded his eye so much. Aaron may remember his eye patch. Father had a strong Boston accent, even worse than mine. I grew up in South Boston if you didn't know." Dr. Blake replied, "Yeah, I know Mel. Is there anything else to mention from that day?" Mel said, "Oh I don't know." Dr. Blake asked, "What Church? I'd like to look up pictures of the church and Father Gerald." Mel said, "Yes it was St. Mark's on Dublin Boulevard. It is a beautiful part of the city and a gorgeous church. The damn place didn't have air conditioning though and it was hot as blazes. Fans were going full blast and my pants kept sticking to my leg." Dr. Blake found two photos from that day with Father Gerald and one just outside the church on the front steps.

Dr. Blake looked at the clock and hurried him along, "OK I think that is enough on that subject, is there anything else you can think of Mel?" Mel answers, "Ah yeah, we got into a car accident one morning on the way to Aaron's first year check-up." Dr. Blake says, "OK, was there anything significant that Aaron would remember from the accident?" Mel answers, "Well yeah, I broke my wrist and Jackie hit her head on the windshield and got a shiner for about a week. And the funny thing is we slid on some ice and rear ended a State Trooper. He was mad and got out of his car yelling and threatening to give me a ticket for driving too fast for conditions." Dr. Blake asked, "Was Aaron hurt?" Mel answered, "No but he was in his car seat screaming while the trooper was in my window yelling at me. Aaron was secured pretty well in his rear facing child seat, so it probably was just the jolt that woke him from a nap or something. We were probably going 25 MPH, and the ice was preventing us from stopping and BAM! We hit the trooper. They called an ambulance to the scene and Jackie was checked for a concussion and my hand was put in a cast for 2 weeks. It was a slight fracture that healed up pretty well. Jackie's mother showed up and got

Aaron, so he didn't ride in the ambulance or go to the hospital at all. He was fine…. Just shaken up a bit." Dr. Blake jumps in and asks Mel, "What kind of car was it and what color interior and exterior?" Mel answers, "Um…it was my Ford Focus hatchback. We bought it that year in a red exterior and gray interior. It was great on gas mileage but not the greatest on ice. Ha ha."

Dr. Blake said, "OK Mel, I think that is enough on that one. Is there anything else that you can think of before I go?" Mel says, "Yes a few more things that I have thought of, and one of them is our plane ride to Boston. Aaron did not have a good flight. We were going there for the baptism. Aaron took a liking to the stewardess'; however, he did not like being put in his car seat while we took off. He threw a tantrum, and he kept grabbing for his ears, so we thought his ears were popping or something. It drove the kid absolutely mad. We sat by the emergency exit so we had a bit more room than the other passengers but that didn't help our comfort level at all because Aaron was keeping us occupied the whole flight." Dr. Blake jumped in and asked, "Were there any other incidents on the flight?" Mel answered, "Well they wouldn't let us take him out of the car seat until the seatbelt light went off, and Aaron cried that entire time. Then we were allowed to get him out of the seat, and we gave him something to drink and eat so that it helped clear his ears, I think. Then during the landing, we had to strap him back in and he cried the whole way down. Then just as we landed, he shits his pants and smelled the whole cabin really bad. It was so bad the stewardess asked if we could be the first off the plane and not one person argued. HAHA! We took him straight to the bathroom and cleaned him up. Maybe it was just gas most of the flight causing him problems. Ha!"

Dr. Blake says, "OK that seems to be enough for that moment. Anything else, you said you had a couple more." Mel says, "Yes this is the last one. When Anna died, Jackie had a rough time with her being sick and visiting her in the hospital a lot." Dr. Blake asked, "You are talking about Jackie's mother, correct?" Mel said, "Yes, that was her mother and she loved her very much. Anna had a stroke at home and was rushed to the hospital a few weeks after Aaron's first birthday. She was found by a neighbor in her garden barely breathing. She spent like 3 days in ICU, and we all spent quite some time in the hospital those 3 days. After she began to get better, they moved her closer to where she would have therapy and she lasted 2 more weeks before another stroke killed her in her sleep. Jackie's high hopes for her mother's recovery were crushed. It was hard on her for the next few months. She didn't want to do anything and stayed around the house all the time."

Dr. Blake's next question was serious, "Mel, do you remember anything from the hospital that jumps out at you as a memory." Mel thinks for a bit and says, "Yes there were a few items. Her room was nice, and it had a very large stainless-steel cross above the headboard. The nurses wore purple. She missed her dog, so we brought her a stuffed dog that looked like her cocker spaniel. There was an elevator outside her room and Aaron loved to push the button for the floor. Even after he pushed the button he wanted to push more. HAHA!"

Dr. Blake grabs his tape recorder and looks at Mel. He says, "Mel, I think I have enough to get a start here. If there is anything else you remember, write it down and I will try to get a hold of you soon to go over those items if I need it." I will be sharing this tape with your lawyer and if he opposes anything we discussed he will let us both know. But like I said he seemed fine with us talking today." Mel answers, "Thanks for getting me out of my cell for a while and the walk down memory lane was nice. Hope we can do it again soon. Let me know if Aaron remembers any of those moments." Dr. Blake says as he looks at his watch, "this here ends our recording this 5th day of May, two thousand and eleven at 2:48p.m."

Chapter 9

Brickman & Miley Sanders

Aaron was having a bad day to say the least. It was Monday and he stepped on gum on the way to school. His teacher caught him falling asleep at this desk during English class. Sean Brickman had been shooting spitballs at him during Math. At lunch, he dropped his milk on his foot and his shoe was wet. Now during recess, he can see that Brickman was getting his posse together for something and Aaron was sure it would involve him.

Sean Brickman had always bullied Aaron and today was no exception. Sean walked up to Aaron and poked his finger very hard right into Aaron's temple and said, "What is that *beautiful* mind dreaming about today?" Aaron poked back at him with, "Just leave me alone today, Brickman! I don't feel like playing your games!" Brickman decided that he wasn't going to accept that answer and stepped on Aaron's foot and began to mess up his hair. Aaron said, "Come on Sean, leave me alone man!" At that moment Sean backed off and quickly said, "Come on guys he isn't worth our time today. Let's go play kickball."

As the boys were walking away Aaron saw Miley Sanders coming over from the corner of his eye. He made quick to change face, but Miley had already seen that he was upset about something. Those boys weren't sticking around when they saw Miley walking over. She has more wit in her pinky finger than all 4 of those boys put together.

Miley always found Aaron to be vulnerable. Aaron usually talked her out of that judgment but today was not going to be one of those times. The older boys had him off his game along with everything else that happened that day. If he couldn't walk away from a situation in a positive way he would carry the negativity with him all day.

Miley found this to be a perfect time to raise his self-esteem. Aaron was still trying to wipe away the disgust from his face when Miley was close enough to start up a conversation. "Aaron, forget those boys, will you walk with me home today after school? I found something yesterday and I want you to look at it." Aaron answered, "Why does Brickman always have to prove his dominance over the 7th graders?" Miley said, "I don't know. Just ignore him and agree to walk with me home after school." Aaron said, "Sure. Did you say you found something yesterday and you want me to see it? What is it?" Miley said, "I can't tell you now, just meet me after school by the bike racks." Aaron agreed and then the bell rang, and they had to get back to their classes. Aaron couldn't help but watch Miley swing her hair around and jog back to her classmates. At that moment, he wished he was in 8th grade with her, so he could be near her all day.

Chapter 10

Miley's Surprise

Aaron got back to class and the feeling of knowing he would be walking home with Miley made him feel good. He couldn't help but sit there in class and wonder what she had to show him. Before he knew it, three o'clock had come and it was time to see Miley again. He walked out with his class and saw her waiting for him at the large oak tree near the bike racks. She had already spotted him and was smiling. She couldn't wait to show him what she had found in the thickets near Penny's Stream. Most of the visitors to the area thought Penny's Stream was named because people would throw pennies into the stream and make a wish, but the locals know it goes way back to the 1880's when a little girl named Penny fell in during a hard rain and drowned.

As soon as Aaron walked up to her, she said, "Ready? Let's go." Aaron was hard pressed to keep up when he asked her, "So what do you have to show me?" She told him, "Just wait and you will find out." She led him the 4 blocks to the Munson St. Bridge and before they crossed, she started down the east slope that went under the bridge. When they reached the bottom, she turned to the south towards Aaron's neighborhood. They followed Penny's stream until they were almost directly west of Aaron's house. At that point there is a stone path that, if you have enough balance, you can skip across to the other side of the stream. Aaron followed her across and she said, "We are almost there Aaron, you are going to like this." They worked their way up to the rocky sand bar and they were surrounded by thickets. Aaron wasn't lost yet but he knew he would lose himself following Miley without a care in the world. Up ahead there were 4 larger trees, and one was easy enough to climb up. Miley helped Aaron up into the tree because she was about a foot taller than him. Once he was up there, she pointed out what she had brought him there to see. It was an old engraving in the tree made with a knife. It was a heart and inside the heart it was inscribed, "M.C. + J.C. Aaron smiled and Miley told him that she had found it yesterday. Miley asked, "Do you think your dad did it?" Aaron replied, "I'm sure it was. It is their initials, and it is practically right behind my house." This added to the positivity that Aaron felt toward the fact that his father was innocent. He thanked Miley for finding it and he said, "I better get home before Christie starts to wonder where I am." Miley was still smiling and said, "Yeah, I need to get home too." Aaron led them back to their neighborhood and neither of them said anything the whole way back.

Chapter 11

Dr. Jaims' Arrival

Dr. Jaims had just arrived in Seattle from San Francisco and was excited to meet and work with Aaron. He walked into Dr. Blake's office and was greeted by Mrs. Kawley. She was waiting to see those big beautiful brown eyes of his. "Well, hello Dr. Jaims. Dr. Blake has been waiting for you. How was your flight?" she asked. Dr. Jaims looked down at this bag and said, "Not too bad, minus the fact that they had my bag on the wrong luggage carousel. Luckily, after waiting for all of the passengers on my flight to collect their bags there was another flight from L.A. that had just landed, and they were collecting their bags at the same time on the carousel next to ours. I was about to go check with the airline when I looked over at their carousel and it was the final bag being shuffled around their carousel somehow." Mrs. Kawley, while she was somewhat distracted by his handsomeness, was shocked and said, "Well I am glad you found it. Let me call Dr. Blake and let him know you are here." She picked up her phone and told Dr. Blake he was here and hung up. She let Dr. Jaims know that he could head back, and that Dr. Blake was finishing up some paperwork.

Dr. Jaims walked back to Dr. Blake's office and opened the door to walk in but then saw that Dr. Blake was not there. He heard a voice from behind him that said, "Brian, I am down here." Dr. Jaims turned around and walked down the main hall further to the next door. It was open and he saw Thom inside the room. "How are you, Thom?" said Dr. Jaims. Dr. Blake looked up to his old college roommate to see he hadn't changed since the last time he had seen him. "I am doing well Brian. How was your flight?" asked Dr. Blake. Dr. Jaims gave him a look and said, "The usual drama at the airport, but I made it in one piece. I can tell you over dinner." Dr. Blake said, "Alright, let me finish this up and we will head out." Dr. Jaims looked at the display that Dr. Blake was putting together and said, "I see you received my shipment all in one piece and you are putting it together as per my instructions. It should make for a good test for Aaron." Dr. Blake said, "Yes, I had the guys from maintenance set up the empty unit in the room across the hall. I have your boxes marked with "B1" and "B2" in there and I have not opened them yet. I have both units against blank walls that are both painted the same color. I am setting up this unit as per your instructions now. Loading the unit with your Box "A" and I have 2 rows to go." Dr. Jaims said, "Let's leave it for tomorrow and we can go to eat now. I am starving." Dr. Blake agreed so they closed up the office with Mrs. Kawley and went out for dinner.

After they finished their meal Dr. Jaims turned to Dr. Blake and he said, "Well, Thom, how did we get to this point?" Dr. Blake said, "It is a long story, and it all starts with how Mel was convicted." Mel's case took a turn for the worse when his co-worker Angie VanPatton took the stand. They were not prepared for the twist she threw at the defense.

As Dr. Blake tells the story he flashes back to the day he was at the trial to learn more about his new patient, Aaron Casey, that he had already been seeing for the last 3 months.

"Ms. VanPatton, can I call you Angie?" District Attorney Ben Henke asked his first question to Angie VanPatton after she took her oath. Angie answered to the court, "Yes you may." Henke asked, "Now how long were you employed by The Casey Worthington Mitchell Law offices?" Angie answered, "Well I had started in May of 1995 and my last day was June 14th, 2001 so just over 6 years." Henke followed up on that question with, "Did you know Melvin Casey before your first day with the firm?" Angie said, "Yes I met Melvin and Jackie at a few lawyer retirement parties, and we knew each other enough to say hi in passing but not anymore." Henke asked, "How long were you with the firm before you had to work with Melvin?" Angie answered, "Well Mel hired me, so we were re-acquainted during the interview process." Henke asked, "What kind of work did you do there?" Angie answered, "Well I answered phones, greeted the potential clients, and made sure they signed in. I did all the odd secretarial work like posting ads locally, writing letters to clients unrelated to their cases. I also opened the office every morning and got everything up and running for the day like making the coffee and making sure the lights and copier were on for the day. Odds and ends you know?" Henke followed up, "Did you work directly with Melvin Casey at times or was it mostly just general work for the entire office?" Angie answered back, "Mel would give me some work to do for him once in a while, but I mostly helped everyone in the office." Henke continued, "OK Ms. VanPatton at what point did your relationship with Mr. Casey become intimate?" Angie blushed and said, "Well it started at the Company Christmas dinner we had in 1998. Mel sat next to me at the Christmas dinner, and he invited a group of us to come back to his place for a little after party." Henke asked, "Was Mrs. Casey attending this dinner that evening?" Angie replied,

"No she was on a trip with her son to visit her Aunt in Chicago I think." Henke asked, "What were you expecting when you went to his after party at the Casey household?" Angie answered, "My friend Justine from Accounts Payable was going and she was my ride, so I really had no choice. She only wanted to stop for one or two drinks." Henke began to question her further about details of the night. "What happened at the Casey residence when you arrived?" She answered, "Mel had opened his wine cellar and brought up 4 or 5 bottles of his finest wine for us to taste. He had been talking about it all night. It had just arrived from Italy, and he hadn't even opened the case yet. So, Mel and Derek broke open the case and they both poured us a drink." Henke asked, "Who was all there at this point?" Angie said, "It was only me, Justine from Accounting, Mel, and Derek Worthington." Henke asked, "Derek Worthington, the partner at Casey Worthington Mitchell Law Offices? Angie answered, "Yes. A few others were supposed to come but I guess they decided otherwise." Henke says, "OK so you are in the Casey residence, Jacklyn Casey is out of town. From my understanding Derek and Justine are now married, is that correct?" This is where Mel Casey's lawyer, Bryson Willerby, stands up and says, "I object, your honor! This information is irrelevant to the case. Judge Jacob Miles, answers "Sustained, can we get to a point here Mr. Henke." Henke answers, "Yes your honor." And he continues, "So Ms. VanPatton, what happened next?" Angie says, "Well we all poured a drink and then while Derek and Justine went and sat by the fire Mel asked me to come look at something he had down in the cellar. We went down the stairs and his cellar was magnificent. There was a bar for tasting and some lounge chairs. We got comfortable and one thing led to another. We had sexual intercourse that night." Henke followed with, "Did this type of sexual relationship continue beyond this one night?" Angie replied, "We continued working as normal around everyone, but it was probably a few months before we were intimate again. And after that we were together multiple times when Jackie would usually leave town." Henke asked, "Was that often?" Angie answered, "Yes Jackie would have to go to L.A. once a month for The Jonathan Charity. She was a board member, and they had meetings once a month." Henke continued, "OK so once a month you were with Melvin Casey while Jackie was out of town on business. Did she ever get a hint that you and Mel were together? Angie replied, "Yes, once she found my underwear under the bed." Henke asked, "What happened when she found that, I am sure she was furious." Angie answered, "Yes, she was but Melvin told her it must have been Christie, her sister, that left them under the bed because they had just stayed at the house while Mel and Jackie went on a weekend trip. She must have been too embarrassed to ask her sister." Henke asked, "Did you see a future in your relationship with Melvin Casey? Or did you two ever discuss this relationship becoming more than it was?" Angie looked down into her hands and said, "Yes, we had talked about Melvin getting a divorce so we could be together, but he would always tell me to just give it a little longer. He would mention Christmas or a holiday or a birthday to extend his time with her. Finally, I told him it was over unless he left her." Henke interrupted, "When did you tell him this?" Angie replied, "It was the night Jackie was killed." The courtroom let out a loud gasp. Henke asked, "Can you tell us how this conversation went down?" Angie replied, "Yes, we were closing up the office for the night and he was trying to get intimate in the break room with me. I told him that we were through until he left Jackie. I didn't want to continue the relationship, 1: because it was bothering me to be a homewrecker, and two, because he wasn't fulfilling his promise to leave Jackie for me." Henke said, "How did he respond to that?" She answered, "Not well. He told me of an idea he had to get rid of Jackie and I told him he was ridiculous for thinking about that. I told him to man up and leave his wife like all divorced men do that are cheating on their wives." Henke asked, "And what did he say to that?" Angie said, "He told me it was too late that he had already paid a guy. I said, paid a guy for what? And he told me there was a client he had that was on parole for killing a man's wife 15 years ago and he paid him to kill Jackie last week. I said, well if you paid him last week when is he supposed to do it? He told me that tonight was the night." Henke asked her to continue with more details, "Well he had planned for a girl's afternoon for Jackie with her friends to the spa and they were to go to dinner afterwards. This was their early anniversary gift because Jackie was going to be in LA during the actual anniversary date. He said when she got home to get ready for their dinner the guy was going to be in the house. He gave him the code to get there before she got home." Henke asked, "How did you react to this news?" Angie began to cry and said, "I wanted away from him as quickly as possible. I wanted to call the police!" Henke asked, "Why didn't you?" Angie replied, "Because he stopped me and explained that we would be set for life. He would get the insurance money, and we could move to anywhere I wanted and live a lavish life without Jackie." "Then what happened?" Henke asked. "Well, he was being forceful with me and continued to convince me of his plan. I became fearful of my own life and agreed with him. I just wanted to get home so I told him I would go away with him. He told me his next step was to call Christie and Greg Flint to tell them he was running late from the office. He would meet them at the Casey residence to pick up Aaron. The original plan was for them to take Aaron to the Flint household for the night. He was going to ask them to meet him at home so they would find the body of Jackie. He told me he had already gone to the ATM 30 minutes ago at his bank across the street, so he had proof that he was not home at the time of the murder. He would say the money was for their anniversary dinner that night. His plan was well thought out." Henke asked, "Then what happened?" Angie said, "Well that was about it, he told me to lay low for the weekend and he would try to contact me on Monday. I did just that and did not tell anyone anything until today." Henke said, "That is all I have at this time, your honor."

The Judge looked over at Willerby and asked him to cross-examine the witness. Willerby asked, "Didn't the police ever question you?" Angie answered, "Yes, but they only asked me if I had worked with Mel and if he was stressed at work up until the murders. I just answered, Yes, I had worked with him and no that he seemed fine to me during work hours. They became distracted and then never came back to my house." Willerby asked, "Well how did they become distracted?" Angie said, "Some kids drove by in the back of their pickup truck and egged their police car and they gave chase and never came back. I am guessing they did not see any other reason to question me." Willerby said, "OK well my next question is, why did you not go to the police with your story?" Angie answered, "Well Mr. Willerby, that is because Melvin came to me one morning as I opened the office. He told me to stay quiet or he would kill my daughter. She lives down in Portland with her dad and he threatened to have her killed whether he was in jail or not and after seeing what he did to Jackie I believed he was not bluffing when he said that." Mr. Willerby followed up, "Well doesn't that make you scared today telling the story?" Angie teared up and answered, "Yes but I have felt guilty for what I did to Jackie, and I cannot live with myself anymore. The truth needs to be known. Melvin needs to be punished for what he did."

Dr. Jaims was listening intently to Dr. Blake's story when he decided to interrupt with a question. "Did Mel ever take the stand in this case?" Dr. Blake answered, "Yes, he did, and he denied everything; however, he did admit to being with Angie the night of the Christmas party in 1998. He called it a mistake, but the jury may have painted him as an adulterer at that point and it possibly put some doubt in their minds as to how far he would take the relationship. He said it ended after that party and did not continue but I think some of them thought he was lying. He admitted to going to the ATM for the dinner money and about closing the office late. The phone call to the Flint household was on his phone records just as Angie explained. The dots to Angie's story all connected. Jackie's neck was broken, and she was thrown down the stairs so it looked like an accident. Her body was found by Greg Flint as he came to the residence to pick up Aaron for the weekend. You can hear Aaron crying in the background of the 911 call. He was hysterical."

Chapter 12

Aaron's First Test

Aaron was ready for action today. He knew he was to meet Dr. Jaims again for the first time in many years. Christie was yelling upstairs to him, "Hustle it up Aaron or we will be late." He grabbed his journal, and they were on their way. Christie said to Aaron, "Get your seatbelt on. What do you think this new Doctor will have up his sleeve today?" Aaron said, "First off just to remind you his name is Dr. Brian Jaims, one of the most respected therapists in San Francisco." Christie said, "How do you know that?" Aaron said, "Well I looked him up last night on the Internet. I read that he specializes in Alzheimer and Amnesia patients. He is also the President of a clinic for gifted children. They concentrate on memory and eidetic recall. I am excited to see what he has in store for me." Christie was concerned and said, "Aaron if you meet with him and you are not comfortable working with him you can tell me. Even if you don't want to upset Dr. Blake you can tell me. I will make sure you don't do anything you would rather not do." Aaron said, "OK." Then Aaron watched the rain the rest of the way to Dr. Blake's office.

Once they arrived at the office Mrs. Kawley greeted them and directed them both to go right in. The doctors had been waiting for them as they set up the eidetic rehab assignment for the day. Usually, Christie only sees Dr. Blake at the end of the session, but this time he wanted her to get comfortable with Dr. Jaims.

They opened the door to Dr. Blake's office and they walked in to only see Dr. Blake. He was studying the first few assignments for Aaron when they walked in. He looked up and greeted them with excitement. Dr. Blake said, "You know what? I am so proud to have Dr. Jaims here with us for the next couple of weeks. He is very excited to meet with you again, Aaron." Christie spoke up and said, "Yeah, where is this quote, most respected therapist from the San Francisco area?" Dr. Blake chuckled and said, "He is in the other room on a phone call to his office. He will be here in just a few minutes." Just then, they heard the door open and Dr. Jaims appeared. Christie couldn't help but notice that he was a handsomely tall man of Spanish descent. He said, "Good Morning to you Mrs. Flint and Mr. Casey. I am so happy we can all finally meet again." Christie was starting to blush and said, "Yes, Dr. Blake has spoken very highly of you. It is nice to meet you." She reached out and shook his hand. He then reached over and shook

Aaron's hand. Aaron was all smiles. Dr. Jaims said to Aaron, "How are you feeling today, Aaron?" Aaron replied, "Great! I am excited to get started today." Dr. Blake cut in and said, "We need to talk with Christie really quick before we start. Aaron, will you leave me your journal and walk down to the break room. Help yourself to anything you want in there."

Aaron handed over his journal and walked down to the break room. It is a small room with a fridge, and a kitchen area with a round table with 4 chairs. He walked up to the water cooler and grabbed a small drink. Then he felt the need to pee. It was probably the nerves of starting the day. He took a quick stop in the restroom across the hall.

Dr. Blake spoke first, "Christie, have a seat." Dr. Jaims grabbed Aaron's journal and walked around to the side bench and sat down just behind Dr. Blake's desk. He opened the journal and listened to the conversation. Dr. Blake said, "How has Aaron been the last couple weeks with the at home exercises? Has he been taking the herbs, sticking to the earlier bedtime, and looking at those worksheets?" Christie says, "He is doing fine. He takes the herbs as he should, and he finally is used to sleeping more this week. The first week he had a hard time going to sleep an hour earlier than usual, but this week he was definitely getting his sleep. The 6 worksheets, he looked at for 5 minutes each, right after dinner yesterday just as the packet described. He also listened to the CD that was included with the 48 photos. One word for each picture." Dr. Jaims spoke up, "Good. Those 6 worksheets will be a good test for him today. Christie, it is OK for me to call you Christie, right?" Christie felt like she was blushing again and said, "Sure." Dr. Jaims continued, "Christie, I am glad Aaron is cooperating. The hard work will pay off over the next couple of weeks. Dr. Blake has told me how gifted Aaron is and I will be testing that this week before we get into the real reason I am here." Christie asks quickly, "What is the real reason you are here?" Dr. Jaims looked at Dr. Blake and then Christie did too. Dr. Blake said sheepishly, "Christie, I am sorry I haven't disclosed the entire reason we are doing this." Christie was quick to say, "OK, continue!" Dr. Blake said, "I was approached by Detective Jon Roberts of the Seattle Police Department last month. It seems as if the new District Attorney is going over all of the trials that occurred during the time that former D.A. Ben Henke was in office. That spans from January of 1996 to December of 2004. This is based upon the recent indictment that Ben Henke was involved with trial manipulation." Christie was shocked and said, "Ok, well who else knows you are doing this with Aaron, because his safety and well-being are my first priority." Dr. Blake said, "I had a conference call with the D.A., Detective Roberts, and Dr. Jaims last week. I also had a visit with Mr. Casey on Thursday to obtain some information about Aaron's early years. Mr. Casey and his Attorney know about this as well." Christie thinks for a minute and says, "Will Aaron know what he is involved with here?" Dr. Blake says, "Well, the DA would like him to remain unaware of the investigation for as long as possible. I told the DA I would like you to decide what we should tell Aaron. So, what do you think?" Christie stands up and says, "I think you guys are nuts! Aaron is smart enough to figure it out!" Dr. Jaims cuts in, "How about we get through this week of testing while you think about how we can gently bring it to Aaron's attention?" Christie says, "That is fine, but if he asks me, I will not lie to him." The doctors agree and ask Christie if she would like to stay for the first test. She says, "That is fine. You two have me interested."

Dr. Jaims goes out to the hallway and walks down to the break room. Aaron is there doodling on a piece of paper. Dr. Jaims looks at what he was drawing, and it looks like a tree carving. A heart with M.C. + J.C. and Dr. Jaims says, "Hey, I saw that in your journal. What is it?" Aaron said, "Oh, it's just something I found carved in a tree behind my house." Dr. Jaims asks, "Do you think M.C. is your father?" Aaron says, "I doubt that it's a coincidence. I am sure it was him." Dr. Jaims says, "Alright, well we are ready for you now."

Once everyone is in Dr. Blake's office, Dr. Blake starts off the conversation. "I'm going to let Dr. Jaims take over from here. He will guide us through the first test." Dr. Jaims jumps right in and starts his first test, "Aaron, one of the main techniques we will be practicing is photo elicitation. This is where the human brain is sparked by photos that are either similar or exact to a given situation. Later today we will let you study a scene for an allotted amount of time and then we will see if you can replicate the scene. If you get stuck, we will use photo elicitation to see how you respond. This will give us a baseline for how this technique will work in live situations. Two weeks ago, with Dr. Blake, he took you on a walk, am I correct? Aaron said, "Yeah, the one across the street? How did you know that?" Dr. Blake interrupts, "This was part of your first assignment, Aaron. I couldn't tell you or it would ruin the test." Dr. Jaims continues, "Dr. Blake recorded your conversation, and we have taken photos of almost every crack and turn of this choreographed walk. Now Aaron, do you remember how long the walk was?" Aaron thinks back and answers, "I have no idea." Dr. Jaims says, "Go ahead and just give a guess." Aaron gives a guess, "Twenty-five minutes?" Dr. Jaims says, "Close enough. We have it down as 27 minutes and 21 seconds. Do you remember what your conversation was about?" Aaron answers quickly, "Yes. It was about some photographs." Dr. Jaims says, "Yes. I need you to take a look over at this table next to us. I have set up the 7 pictures on the table and I need you to put them in the order in which you had seen them on the walk."

Dr. Blake walks over and takes the tablecloth off the table to reveal the photos in a box and some numbers on the table. Aaron gets up and walks over to the table. In the 4 or 5 seconds it takes him to walk over to the tables he is already sure he can put them in order. They were very different scenes. First there was a photo of a farm. He flipped through the box of photos and found the farm. Dr. Jaims said, "Go ahead and set it on the paper that says Number 1. Now, you can look for the remaining photos and put them in order on the table." Aaron continues looking through the photos, and he finds the second photo. It is a homeless man on the street. Aaron sets it on the table covering a paper saying Number 2 and goes back to find the third photo. As he starts to look through the photos, he sees that there is another photo of the farm. His selection for photo number 1 is there twice. At this point in time, he realizes that there are about 20 photos left and only 5 more spots on the table. He looked up at Dr. Jaims, who was watching him intensely and said, "There is another photo of the farm." Dr. Jaims said, "Look at it closely. They are not the same photo. I need the correct photo on the table." Aaron looked over at Dr. Blake and Dr. Blake said, "Nobody said these tests were going to be easy Bud." Christie was standing next to Dr. Blake and she started to chuckle. Aaron turned back to the box of photos and was determined to get this table filled correctly. He took another look at the new farm photo he had just discovered. It was filled with silos, a big barn, some trucks hauling corn, and then Aaron noticed the tractor was missing from the shot. He closed his eyes and imagined the walk he took with Dr. Blake just two weeks earlier and remembered that Dr. Blake made a point to mention the tractor. It was a John Deere and Dr. Blake said he loved old tractors. He set the photo with the missing tractor on the floor under the table. Aaron decided that he would look through the pictures and find the seven in order quickly and

then look at the differences in the photos. He
found the other homeless man's photo and set it
on top of the one already on the table. He moved
on to the next photo to which he remembered was
a tiger in a zoo enclosure. He found 3 photos of
that one and he set them down and moved on to
the fourth photo. He found two photos of the
Eiffel Tower and set them down in their place.
Three more photos to go. Aaron gave it a thought
and saw the next photo staring him in the face. It
was the Golden Gate Bridge. He set the photos on
the table and looked up at Dr. Jaims to see that he
was smiling. Dr. Jaims said, "I picked that one."
Aaron stepped back to the box and pulled all the
photos out and set the two photos of a
hummingbird down on number 6. The remaining 2
photos were of a waterfall. Now that Aaron was
satisfied with the order he walked over to the
photos of the homeless man. He saw that he was
on a bus stop bench covered up with a blanket. It
looked like fall or wintertime. The man had a
winter cap on and gloves. That is when Aaron
realized the differences. He saw that in one photo
the man had the fingers cut out of his gloves. This,
obviously, was the correct photo. Aaron
remembered the gloves stuck out in the photo to
him, because the fingers were cut out. He set the
incorrect photo back in the box and moved it to

photo 3. This was the Tiger photo. There were 3 in this set. He made a quick elimination because one of the photos was black and white. He remembers this photo being in color. However, when he looked at the other two, they both seemed incorrect. One had a second tiger in the background. Aaron didn't remember this in the walk from two weeks ago. The other photo was wrong because there was a sign missing that said, "Do not climb on the enclosure." At this point he looked up at Dr. Jaims. Dr. Jaims said, "Pick the photo closest to being correct. Aaron picked up the black and white photo and it was exactly as he remembered minus the color. He sat the black and white photo on the table and moved on to the next photo. Christie looked over at Dr. Blake and gave him an elbow. Dr. Blake whispered to her, "We will explain that one later." Next up was the Eiffel Tower. This was a tourist photo with 3 tourists standing in a pose. In one photo the tower is dead center over the man in the middle, and in the other photo the tower is to the left. Aaron doesn't remember concentrating that hard on this photo. He closed his eyes and thought back to a couple weeks ago. Dr. Blake mentioned that this photo was of his brother, and that is when he pointed right at his brother. Aaron thought hard about this point in the conversation and when he looked harder at Dr. Blake's brother. He is pretty sure the tower was centered over his brother in the middle of the 3 tourists. He sat that photo on the table and the other in the box. He moved on to the next photo. This was the Golden Gate Bridge. Dr. Jaims spoke up and said, "Good Luck on this one Aaron, I actually use this one on my students back home." Aaron looked at the photos hard. The photos did have a few differences. The three photos were of the same angle of the bridge but seemed to be on different days or different times of the day. They all showed the full expanse of the bridge. You can see the city, and the water on a beautiful day. With his doubt about getting this photo correct he thinks back to his walk with Dr. Blake two weeks prior. They glanced at this photo without conversation and walked to the next photo. Aaron had no clue, so he set those photos down and moved on to the next. Aaron picked up the Hummingbird photos and thought OK, two left. That's when Aaron remembered there was an eighth photo. Well, it wasn't really a photo but more of a drawing or sketch. He looked up at Dr. Jaims and asked, "Wasn't there one more photo down this hallway?" Dr. Jaims responds, "Yes there was Aaron. Once you are done with this test that will be your next test. Let's concentrate on these last two photos first and then we will move on to that test." So, Aaron continued. He looked down at the Hummingbirds and saw that one was green, and the other was pinkish in color. They were the same exact photo, just different colored birds. The green bird was easily the correct photo. He set it down and moved it to the last photo. The last photo was the waterfall. He could see that these photos were almost similar. The water was falling from a small stream over a small drop. The drop was about 15 feet, and you could see both the top of the waterfall and the stream below. It looked as if the photo was taken from a large tree on the lower side of the falls. Since he had no idea what the difference was, just by glance, he thought back to the walk with Dr. Blake a couple weeks earlier. He remembered that Dr. Blake pointed out a small deer at the top side of the waterfall in the brush. He looked at the photos and the deer was there in both photos. He couldn't remember anything else from the conversation on the walk. He looked closer at the deer and noticed that one had a small set of antlers, and the other was without antlers. This is when he remembered that Dr. Blake referred to the deer as a "button buck" when they walked away from the photo. He instantly put the correct photo in its place and walked back to the golden gate bridge photos. He held them up and was totally stumped. He did notice that each photo was shot from a slightly different angle, but not enough to decide which photo was correct. He looked at the bridge details comparing each one. Dr. Jaims steps up to the table and can sense that Aaron is having trouble. He looks at the table and tells Aaron, "Well Aaron, I can tell you that all the other pictures you have are correct. This one looks to be giving you trouble." Aaron says, "Yeah, a little bit." Dr. Jaims says, "Think back to your walk. How did the conversation in this picture go down?" Aaron laughed and said, "It didn't go down at all." Dr. Jaims looked over at Dr. Blake for help. Dr. Blake stepped up to the table now too. Christie looked concerned. Dr. Blake said, "Think back, Aaron." Aaron closed his eyes. He did remember that at some point of the walk Dr. Blake muffled a word under his breath. It sounded like "House lamps." Aaron thought back and said it out loud quietly. "House lamps." Dr. Blake said, "That is close, try again. Think hard." Aaron said, "White Naps?" Dr. Jaims said, "No, look at the photos now, while you think of what he said." Aaron yelled, "White CAPS!" Aaron looked at the 3 photos and only one of the photos had white caps on the water. He put 2 incorrect photos on the ground under the table and put the last photo in place.

Dr. Jaims said, "Great memory! In this test, we needed to see that the photos would spark your elicitation of the things around you. Sounds and sights work together to form one memory of a situation. It is like hearing a song on the radio and it takes you back to a time in your life where you can almost vividly see the actions that took place in that time and space. The next test will push that to the next level." Dr. Jaims continues, "Do you remember that mural on the building you have already mentioned at the end of the walk?" Dr. Blake walks in carrying an easel and some drawing paper. Aaron replies, "Yes." Dr. Blake asks, "Can you draw that here on the easel?" Aaron says, "I can try." He grabs the marker and begins to draw an old chevy bel air with a gas station pump next to it and a service station behind. Dr. Jaims is actually very impressed by how many details Aaron remembers from this sketch down to the type of hub caps on the car and the brand of the fuel pump with the company logo of a dinosaur.

As Aaron is drawing, he is remembering the smell they encountered as they were walking past this sketch. It was a burned rubber smell. Christie can see him pause and she asks Aaron, "What is it, honey?" Aaron says, "Well I remember there was a terrible rubber smell as we walked by this sketch." Dr. Blake laughs and says, "HAHA yes that is part of the test here today, Aaron. It was all a stunt to help you remember." Aaron turns to Dr. Blake with pressed lips and says, "THAT was added to spark my memory? It had a terrible smell!" Dr. Blake says, "OK Aaron, this was an ad and there was a phone number for the service station at the bottom of the page. Can you remember the number?" Aaron was a bit stumped and said, "There was parentheses where the area code was, and I can picture that and now I can picture those 3 numbers. It was (866) but the remainder is not coming to me. Wait, there was a 484 after that. (866) 484- and I am stumped again after that." Dr. Jaims jumps in, "Aaron, can you write what you have so far on the board, and we will try to determine the last four numbers with a technique I have coined, "S.A.T." and that stands for "Smell Association Trigger." With an SAT test, it is exactly what the doctor ordered. We will introduce a smell to spark the memory of that situation." Dr. Blake pulls out a balloon filled with the rubber smell and says, "I will release this odor and with your eyes closed I hope it will help you to discover those last 4 digits. Take a good look at the sketch for about 10 seconds and think back to the walk. When you close your eyes, I will release the smell, and we will see if you can elicit the mural more vividly." Aaron was remembering walking up to the mural and remembers a small sound of air release which must have been when they released the smell. Aaron closes his eyes to think a little harder about that moment in time. As he heard that sound he turned to see where the smell was coming from and looked at the mural in his memory. He can see the numbers!!!! 4321!!!! Aaron yells out, "I can see it! I can see it! 4321, it's 4321!" Aaron runs over to the sketch and puts 4321 on the board! He is so excited that he could reveal something like that in his memory banks. Dr. Jaims says, "OK let's go to the other room and get away from this smell!" And they all laugh and agree to move quickly to the other room.

Once in the other room they all sat down and took a break. Dr. Jaims says, "Aaron, good work! I want you to know that it was truly amazing. It usually takes me 8 to 10 sessions before I can get results like that. You are truly gifted with your brain just as Dr. Blake has told me." Christie says, "Dr. Blake and Aaron have been working very hard on harnessing what some have called a gift that Aaron has been given with his memory. Dr. Jaims continues, "Aaron there was something from earlier I wanted to explain. The Tiger in the photo was black and white. Studies have shown that color is not as important in eidetic recall as much as the shapes or objects in a photo. We needed to make sure this was proven in your test. It seems as if it was not a factor in getting that photo correct. And this is just as we suspected." Dr. Blake jumps into the conversation here, "I think that is enough testing for today." Dr. Jaims says, "Yes, we can work those photos we gave you with the soundtracks on your next visit. Thank you for your time and make sure you continue to follow the schedule we set out for you in the notebook. It is important for us to reach the next level in this treatment." Christie and Aaron agree, and they head home for the night.

After Aaron and Christie leave testing day number one, Dr. Blake walks over to the session room and begins to clean up. Dr. Jaims looks over at him and says, "I'm going to use the restroom quickly. Do you have Aaron's file somewhere? I would like to study it some more." Dr. Blake is kneeling on the ground putting photos into the storage box and he looks up to Dr. Jaims and says, "Yes, it is on the desk in my office." Dr. Jaims says, "Ok I will be right back." Dr. Blake stands up and puts the box of photos up on the table. He looks over by the corner to where he has a few chairs set up and sees the deflated balloon on the end table. He goes over to pick it up and takes a whiff of the torn end. He says out loud to himself, "Oof, that is a terrible smell. I can't believe we did that to him, and it worked." Dr. Jaims is still on his way out of the room and says, "S.A.T. works every time!"

They both look at each other and laugh. After about 10 minutes Dr. Jaims walks back into the session room and says, "Hey Thom, I was just looking at the original hard file here that you have on Aaron. Why didn't you tell me that he has Synesthesia?" Dr. Blake says, "Yes, that was something we discovered with Aaron years ago when I was beginning his spelling bee training. I had flash cards with spelling words I would use when he was four or five. The cards were a different color for each beginning letter. The main colors were based on the first letter of the word. So, Y was Yellow, and B was blue. The other words were off tones from the primary colors like C was Cyan." Dr. Jaims asked, "Well how did this make you investigate the Synesthesia diagnosis?" Dr. Blake says, "Well I think this spelling practice, along with his eidetic memory, linked words with colors and it drove his mind into other avenues. He began to see colors when he would see or hear the word he had associated with that color. For example, when he hears music it has a dark red tone, or maroon, for him. MUSIC was a maroon-colored card when we trained during his lesson." Dr. Jaims says, "This is very interesting. Do you still have that set of cards?" Dr. Blake says, "I don't think so, but there may be a few floating around here somewhere. You know Synesthesia was a conduit to his eidetic memory discovery. Once I noticed he was gifted with Synesthesia we began to challenge his mind with other things and his eidetic memory became more apparent." Dr. Jaims concluded, "We need to find a way to fit this in our next round of testing with Aaron."

Chapter 13

Miley's Campout!

Miley's just a kid. Her hair is a dirty blonde, with a scrunchy always holding it back into a ponytail. Her bangs are cut straight across just above her eyebrows. She has a twinkle in her eye whenever she is in the company of Aaron. She has what she refers to as, "a feel bad for the fella," crush on him. She defends him whenever the opportunity is to present itself. She has a cozy little spot for him in her heart. To some she won't admit this crush, mentioning her mom, and brothers. She speaks the truth of this crush only to her father. That's right; Miley is a Daddy's girl. He can read her like a book, and the same goes likewise. Miley's dad is a bit of an outdoorsman. He loves to fish, hunt, and just be with nature. When Miley was very young, he would pitch the tent in the backyard and have a fire with her. They would make s'mores or toasted jellies and tell stories. As Miley got older, he would still set up the tent for her a couple times in the summer. Miley would invite a friend, and her dad would man the fire until bedtime. He would put out the fire and say lights out girls and head into bed with Mrs. Sanders.

Tonight was a similar night, but she had invited Aaron along with her friend Ashley. Miley's dad was fine with Aaron being there if Miley had one of her girlfriends there too. So, they made toasted Jellies and camped by the fire. Her dad told a few stories, and it was time for lights out. Ashley, Miley, and Aaron climbed in the tent and bundled up in sleeping bags. Usually, Miley took keep of the flashlight. After Dad went into the house, she would prop the flashlight up to shine on the ceiling of the tent. This would create an ambient light throughout the tent. She learned this trick from her dad.

She got the light set up in the tent and said, "Let's play truth or dare." Aaron said, "OK, I will go first. Dare!" Miley said, "OK, you have to take off your shirt and run across the street and touch the neighbor's light pole, yell like a chicken, and run back." Aaron said, "OK." He took off his shirt, unzipped the tent and began to run to Miley's side gate. The girls followed him to hold the gate open. As they laughed hysterically, he ran as fast as he could and touched the light pole in the front yard and yelled, "Cock-a-doodle doo." He started to run back when he saw the headlights of a car coming. He ran across the street and the car honked. He got back to the gate and the girls and Aaron jumped into the tent and zipped it up. They were laughing hysterically in the tent as Aaron put his shirt back on. Miley said, "OK, it's my turn. Truth!" Ashley jumps into the game and says, "OK Miley, have you ever had a crush on any of the boys at school." Aaron's ears perked up quickly on this one. He wants to know how she will answer this question. He can hear his heart start to beat a little faster even though it was on its way down from his shirtless run. Miley smiles and says, "Well I hate to admit this but back in 4th grade I used to have a crush on Sean." As Aaron's eyes balloon up to the size of quarters Ashley says, "Are you kidding me! Brickman! That kid is a total jerk!" Miley was quick to defend it, "I know, I know he is a jerk now but back then he was kind of sweet. I think his parents getting divorced changed his attitude on life a bit, so I totally hate his guts now." Ashley said, "Good. Do you want to know who my crush is?" Miley said, "Hey, you will get your turn at the game next. Haha." Aaron all the sudden feels like a knife is stabbed into his heart. Brickman is a dweeb. The kid is intolerable and a menace to our community. He hopes it is all in the past and something she has moved on from. Miley speaks up, "OK Ashley it is your turn. Truth or Dare?" Ashley says, "Truth and you have to ask me about my crush!" Miley says, "OK, who is your crush?" Ashley's eyes light up and she says in her most excited voice, "JOSH Damian!" Miley says, "Eeew, gross. He used to eat glue at our table in kindergarten!" Ashley says, "Well he doesn't eat glue now. He has matured into a hunk-a-hunk-a burning love." Miley says, "Oh my god, where did you hear that?" Ashley says, "My aunt always says that when we watch wrestling on TV and Ricco Swavey makes his entrance." Miley says, "OK Aaron your turn again." Aaron looks down and says, "I really don't want to play anymore." Miley says, "Well I have a good one for you if you take Truth." Aaron says, "OK truth." Miley says, "What is the farthest back you can remember with that great memory of yours?" Aaron doesn't really want to answer this one, but he says, "Well my mom died when I was two and a half. I still remember her. She always would laugh when I said truck because my TR sounded like F and I would say fruck." Ashley said, "You were there when she died, right?" Aaron said, "Yes but that day only comes to me in dreams." Ashley said, "Tommy told me that your dad killed your mom." Aaron glared over at her and said, "That isn't true. At least, I don't think it's true. I try not to think about it much because I am scared, I may know who the killer really was." Ashley pried some more, "Well your dad is in prison, isn't he?" Aaron looks at her again with pressed lips, "Yes but Dr.

Blake told me he could help me remember that day my mother died, and I hope I can remember who it was that killed her. I don't believe it was my dad. I know a lot of people that don't believe it either." Miley decides to change the subject. She announces, "OK it is my turn, and I choose dare this time." Aaron laughs and says, "OK well I would like to see you jump on one leg over to the fence and back while holding the flashlight, barefoot." Ashley laughed and said, "Yeah that would be hilarious and with each hop you have to recite the alphabet." Miley grabbed the flashlight and took off her socks. She grabbed the flashlight and said, "Here I go. A- B- C- D- E- F- G-" At that moment, her foot hit a muddy spot, and she slipped onto her butt and began to laugh wildly! She grabbed the flashlight, touched the fence and ran back to the tent.

Once again, they were all in the tent laughing until their stomachs hurt. Then they heard one of the windows open from the house and Miley's dad yelled, "Lights OUT campers!" That was Miley's dad's way of saying time for bed. Miley looked over at Aaron and said, "I guess we can be finished. That was super fun though." Ashley agreed and they shut off the light and got comfortable in their sleeping bags. Aaron said, "Good night girls." Ashley said, "Sorry to bring up your mom and dad earlier and I hope Dr. Blake can help you remember." Miley said, "Same here Aaron, good night."

Chapter 14

Car Ride to the Baseball Game

Greg Flint sees Aaron walking up the front sidewalk from his sleep over. Greg yells, "Hey Aaron, ready to go or we're going to be late? I'll grab the bat bag and baseballs and meet you in the car." Greg looks over to Christie on the front porch and says, "Let's hit the road, Babe. We got a game to play." Christie says, "I know, let me get my shoes and I'll meet you in the car."

Once they run out to the car they head to the game. Christie looks at the back seat and sees Aaron putting his baseball hat on. She says to him, "That was a very interesting day at Dr. Blake's office. I really like Dr. Jaims. He's a very smart man. Aaron replies, "I told you he's one of the best doctors on the west coast." Christie looks over at Greg and says, "Honey, you should have seen the test they did with Aaron the other day. They had all these pictures set out on the table and Aaron had to choose the correct one. They were pictures that Aaron had seen two weeks earlier on a walk with Dr. Blake. Aaron got them all right." Greg says, "That's great. I'm really trying to think about this game. I need to fix the lineup when we get there. I will probably have to sit Aaron and Stan first. But I'll make sure to get him in the game by the fourth inning." Christie looks over at Greg and says, "You're going to sit him another game?" Aaron sits up and says, "It's okay Aunt Christie, we have to win this to get to the city championship." Christie says, "Okay, as long as you're okay with it. Now back to Dr. Jaims. What do you think he'll do next Aaron?" Aaron looks out the window and he says, "Well, I heard they went and talked to Dad and that you gave them some of mom's old photo albums. So, I think it has something to do with the time before mom died." Greg looks over at Christie and says, "What are these quacks doing now? Why do they have to dig so deep into the past? The past is over, we all need to just move on." Christie looks at him and says, "Well you can't always shut out the past. You can't just bottle it up and be done with it like that. We need someone there for us to talk about it and move on after that. They have never covered the early years with Aaron before because he could never remember, so now they're trying to see if he can remember anything from those years so he can move on and push to the next level."

They make it to the baseball field and Greg says, "Okay. We're here. We can talk about this later. Hey Slugger, meet me at the back of the car to grab the baseballs." Once they get around to the back of the car, Greg sees Christie walking toward the bleachers, and he grabs Aaron by the shoulders. He says, "Hey Slugger, listen we got to get a big win tonight. Don't let that Dr. Blake stuff get in your head, okay? It's just you and the baseball diamond. I know sometimes you daydream out in the Outfield, but we got to pay attention tonight." Aaron agrees and they walk the equipment to the field.

Chapter 15

The Baseball Game

It was the bottom of the fourth inning and Greg was walking in from coaching third base. He yelled from home plate, "Hey Aaron, you're going to right field this inning." Aaron jumped up quickly and grabbed his glove to run out. Greg saw he was missing his hat and said, "Hey slugger, don't forget your hat!" Aaron said, "Oh yeah, I almost forgot." He grabbed his hat and ran out to right field. Once he got out there the centerfielder Johnny was in motion to throw him a pop up to warm up before the inning was to start. Aaron got under the ball and watched the ball drop to the ground right next to him. He ran over, picked up the ball, and threw it back to Johnny. His throw came up short by about 3 feet and Johnny scooped it up and threw it to left field.

While waiting for his turn Aaron really had his mind on Miley and the truth or dare game from the other night. Did she really have a crush on Brickman? Man, he hated that kid with a passion even before this new information became known to him. Now to find out she really kind of liked the kid back in 4th grade made Aaron a little jealous. Suddenly Aaron heard Johnny yell, "Heads up, Aaron." Just as he snapped out of it, he had enough time to snag the fly ball. As he caught it, he heard the catcher yell, "Balls in, coming down!" So, Aaron took his best aim and threw the ball into the dugout. Greg came out and picked up the balls so the inning could begin.

Aaron took his position and waited for the pitch. "Strike one!" The Umpire said. Aaron was glad that Tommy was pitching because not a lot of kids could hit Tommy's fast ball. "Strike Two," the umpire erupted. The kid wasn't even swinging the bat. Aaron looked down and kicked the dirt out of boredom. He looked back up and heard, "Strike Three you're out!" Aaron yelled, "Yes! Nice pitch Tommy!" The next batter came up and was a lefty. Greg yelled out to Aaron, "Be ready, Aaron. We have a lefty up." Aaron yelled back, "OK!" Then he waved his throwing hand, so Greg knew he was paying attention.

Just as his arm fell to his side, he started to think of Miley again. Maybe it was that he needed a distraction from the baseball game that made him nervous. Thinking of Miley made him calm down. He wasn't sure but it didn't help when the ball was hit to him. He wondered what she was doing right at that moment. "Strike ONE!" He heard from the umpire, and he went right back to thinking of Miley. Boy, he really had fun at the campout the other night. Running around the yard with his shirt off was hilarious. Then having Miley jump on one leg to the fence and back was a riot.

That is when Aaron heard the crack of the bat. The ball was coming in his direction. It was a ground ball that got through the infield. He ran over to get the ball, and it went right through his legs. Luckily, Johnny was backing him up and grabbed the ball and threw it into 2nd base, but the kid was safe at 2nd with a double. Aaron hit his glove and Tommy looked disappointed in him from the pitcher's mound. Johnny said, "Nice try Aaron. Better luck next time."

He went back to his dirt hole in the grass of right field where all the kids stood all summer and waited for the next batter. This time he decided to distract himself with thoughts of what was happening with Dr. Blake and his new sessions with Dr. Jaims. Will he reach new levels with his memory with Dr. Jaims? What is the plan with this new rehab therapy? Little does Aaron know that they will test his mental abilities to levels most people have never achieved. Dr. Jaims is a brilliant man but even more brilliant with the right patient to work with. That is when Aaron heard the umpire yell, "Strike Three!" The half inning was over, and Aaron ran into the dugout with the rest of his team. He couldn't help but wonder if he would get a chance to bat this inning.

Once in the dugout he set down his glove and hat and asked Greg, "Where am I in the line-up?" Greg told him, "You are up 3rd this inning." Great, that means he will definitely get to bat even if the first two kids get out. He walked over and grabbed his helmet and his bat. Tommy was up next, and Johnny was on deck. That put Aaron in the hole waiting to get on deck next. Tommy swung at the first 3 pitches and was called out. Johnny was up and that put Aaron out on deck. This is when he always gets nervous. He looked over at the bleachers to see his Aunt Christie eating popcorn and talking to Josie, Johnny's mom. Aaron went back to swinging the bat. He started to think of Miley again. He wished she would come to his games. This one time when he played on the smaller field, he remembered that she was there with her friend from girl scouts. It was Megan, and she had a twin brother the same age as Aaron. Megan moved to Dallas the next year and that ended Miley's visits to the ball diamonds. So, he didn't expect Miley to ever show up to one of his games.

"Strike Three!" yelled the umpire. Johnny went down on 3 swings just like Tommy. "Man, this pitcher must be on tonight," Aaron thought. Aaron tightened his batting glove and walked up to the plate. He looked down at Greg on 3rd base and no sign was given. Greg just said, "Let's go Aaron, start us off!" Aaron got in the batter's box and took the first pitch. "Strike One!" He shook his head yes as to tell the pitcher good pitch and to let the umpire know, "Yes, I agree with you on that call." He watched the 2nd one go right to the catcher's glove and it made a popping sound. POP! "Strike two!!!!" Now Aaron is thinking curve ball. He must throw me the curve ball because if it goes in the dirt and it is ball one it is no big deal. So, Aaron chokes up on the bat a bit, something that Greg tells him to do with 2 strikes. He scoots up in the box, something else that Greg tells him to do when he thinks the curve ball is coming. And he sees the pitcher agree with the catcher on the sign. He sees the pitcher digging in his glove a bit. This was another indication to Aaron that the curve ball was coming. The pitcher winds up and throws the ball. Just as Aaron expected from his lessons with Greg over the years, it is a curveball. He picks up the spin on the ball and takes an early swing to connect with the ball before it starts to break too much. Before he knows it, he has connected with the ball and it is sent out to the short outfield right before the outfielders can reach it and he is safe at first.

Greg yells over, "That a boy, nice hit slugger!" He is excited to be on first and he looks over to Christie in the bleachers and she is standing up and clapping wildly and she yells, "Nice hit, Aaron!!!" After Aaron, in the line-up, is a kid named Stan. Greg always calls him "Stan the Man" but the kids on the team call him, "Stan the Garbage Man." Stan was from the lower-class part of town and was always ridiculed for that. 3 straight pitches and Stan was out.

Aaron ran back to the dugout where Christie was waiting and she told him, "Great hit, Aaron." Greg came into the dugout too and said, "Way to pick up on that curve ball kid! Now get out to Right Field and don't miss any grounders like last inning. Johnny won't be there to back you up every time." They went on to win the game 3-2 and Greg was happy because this game put them in as the top seed in the city tournament after the weekend.

Chapter 16

Detective Roberts Visits Christie

Detective Jon Roberts is starting his day by stopping by the Flint Household. He parks his police car on the street and walks up to the door. He rings the doorbell and Aaron answers the door. Detective Roberts speaks first, "Hello, I am here to speak with Christie Flint, is she home?" Aaron says, "Yes, stay here. I will go get her for you." Aaron runs back to the table where his bowl of cereal was getting soggy and says to Christie, "It wasn't Miley like I thought. It is a man for you, Aunt Christie." She says, "For me? OK I will go see who it is."

Christie walks toward the door and opens it up. She talks through the screen door. "Hi there, can I help you?" The man says, "Hi, I am Detective Jon Roberts of the Seattle Police Department." Christie looks just beyond the detective and sees Miley halfway down the sidewalk. Christie interrupts the detective and says, "Um, hold on." She waves at Miley and says, "Hey Miley, I will tell Aaron you are here." The Detective turns around and looks at Miley. He nods his head at her and says, "Good Morning." Christie turns toward the kitchen and says, "Aaron, Miley is out here waiting for you."

Christie opens the screen door and walks out onto the porch with the detective. Just then Aaron blows through the doorway and shuffles around Christie. He says, "Bye Christie, see you after school!" As he reaches the sidewalk Miley says to him, "Why is there a detective here?" Aaron says, "I don't know, let's go!" Christie looks back at the detective and says, "Sorry it's crazy around here in the mornings. What can I help you with?" Detective Roberts says, "Well I wanted to introduce myself and let you know I will be working with Dr. Blake on the Melvin Casey investigation. We believe that Aaron may be of some help in identifying who really killed your sister Jacklyn." Christie says, "Why is that, because Aaron was in the house when she was killed? He was 2 years old and that was 10 years ago! I really hope you have more evidence to help Melvin than my 11-year-old nephew's eidetic memory. Please tell me more about what you have on the case." The detective looked over at the corner of the porch and said, "Well, our new district attorney has plenty to get us started that I can't talk about at this moment, but Aaron could be our ace in the hole." Christie laughs and says, "Ha, well detective I will give you my best poker face as you leave. There is nothing more we need to discuss unless you have specific questions for me?"

Detective Roberts decides to continue and says, "Well, Dr. Blake will not release any documents to us because of the client doctor confidentiality agreement. So, is there anything you can tell me that the District Attorney would appreciate the work Dr. Blake does with Aaron? I would like to build his confidence at least a little bit when I get back to the office." Christie says, "OK I will give you one little tip. I was there for the first day with the amazing Dr. Jaims. They let me sit in and observe. Aaron was amazing. They got him to remember a random phone number from 2 weeks ago with a burnt rubber smell. They called it the smell association trigger or S.A.T. I had never heard of it before, but it was amazing! That Dr. Jaims is really something. He's easy on the eyes too!" Detective Roberts says, "Burnt Rubber, huh? Sounds interesting. I will pass that on to the DA and the investigation team. Did it seem like they would come up with any breakthroughs with Aaron? Did he say anything about the murders?" Christie said, "No they have not started that type of testing yet. I think they are easing Aaron into getting comfortable with Dr. Jaims."

Detective Roberts says, "OK well I do have one more thing before I leave. He reaches into the inside pocket of his detective jacket and pulls out some papers. He hands them toward Christie and says, "I need you to take a couple days and look over these release forms. I will need you and Greg, as legal guardians of Aaron, to sign them for the DA. It will give us permission to review Dr. Blake's legacy files on Aaron. It will also give us permission to use the information collected on Aaron by Dr. Jaims and the State of California grant he works under. She says, "OK, I will run these by Greg tonight and we will let you know our decision either way." Detective Roberts says, "I will need them by this Friday so keep that in mind. I also have my card in there so contact me with anything you or Greg would like to share on the case." Christie says, "OK, well I must get to Zumba class. So, we will talk soon and I hope you have a good day Detective."

Chapter 17

Overnight Test – Session 1

Dr. Jaims is waiting in the lobby of Dr. Blake's office when Aaron is dropped off for his first overnight test. Dr. Jaims opens the locked door and invites Aaron into the office. Dr. Jaims says, "Hello Aaron, are you ready for a memorable night?" Aaron says, "I sure am!" Dr. Jaims says, "Did Christie drop you off?" Aaron said, "No Greg had to make a run to the auto parts store for his bike, so he dropped me off on his way there." Dr. Jaims points in the direction of the session rooms and tells Aaron, "Well you know the way, so let's go, we are all set up for you already."

They get back to the session room and Dr. Jaims starts his usual setup. He says, "Aaron, we will need you to take up your shirt so we can put these probes on your chest and back. These will monitor your breathing pattern and heartbeat. We can also see when you get into REM sleep. It is after your first session of REM sleep when we will get our best results with communication while you sleep. So, relax, and we need you to lay on your back while you sleep. The room is temperature controlled to stay at 66 degrees Fahrenheit without windows open or fans on. Oh yeah, I almost forgot. I need you to wear these pupil size detection glasses for collecting some data." Aaron says, "OK cool!" Dr. Jaims watches him put them on and says, "We will be back to check on you in 10 minutes or so." Dr. Blake and Dr. Jaims left the room and went back to the break room for a cup of coffee. Dr. Blake said, "This will be a long night." Dr. Jaims replies, "Usually the first night is not a huge breakthrough, but the second is a bit better when the body and mind is used to being asked to communicate with the conscious."

After a few more minutes, Dr. Jaims decides to check on Aaron. He enters the room and sees that Aaron is very comfortable. Dr. Jaims sits down in the chair next to Aaron's bed and says, "To keep with your usual nightly routine we will now do your cards. However, we will be flashing the cards on the ceiling, and you will have to be the one announcing the word that is associated with the card. Are you ready to begin Aaron?" Aaron turns his head to look at Dr. Jaims and says, "Sure." Dr. Blake says from the projector where he can flip the slides, "We will now turn off the lights and we will flash the pictures on the ceiling......we need you to say the word that is mentioned on the CD track we gave with the photos." Dr. Blake takes the remote and clicks forward one slide. Photo one is flashed on the ceiling, it is a photo of a meadow full of grass. Aaron says, "PICKLE!" The next slide is put on the ceiling, and he yells, "Baseball." This was a photo of a football player. Aaron also says, "I always wondered why it said baseball when it was a football player." Dr. Jaims says, "Many of these items are similar but not exact just to add some complexity, Aaron." The next photo flashes and it is a tiger. Aaron yells, "Jungle." The next three flash: a monkey, a window with bars, and a pineapple. Aaron answers quickly in order as they flashed, "Trees, Theft, Sweet." The next picture threw Aaron for a loop. It showed a lady carrying two large paper grocery bags, one in each arm, and it was familiar to Aaron, but it was a photo taken of the lady's backside. Normally when he saw this photo it was taken on her front side with the bags. Aaron hesitantly yelled, "Ahh…List?" Dr. Blake answered, "Yes that is correct. This photo was a test for you Aaron. Like we have described to you earlier, photo elicitation has proven to be effective with partial scenes and even similar scenes. This photo from another angle than you are used to seeing is still linked in your brain to the word, List. This evidence bodes well for our future projects in stemming your memories of the past." Flash, the next photo is of a bridge over a small creek. Aaron, without thinking, says, "cold." Dr. Jaims says, "Wow Aaron you are doing great. Let's continue." The next picture to flash on the ceiling is of a zoomed image of a fly on a wall. "Green!" Aaron speaks to this one easily with the wall being green and the fly's red bug eyes.

This imagery continues for the next 20 minutes, and Aaron becomes very tired. This is his typical night routine, so his mind and body have relaxed as if it was his usual bedtime. Dr. Jaims says to Aaron, "Now usually my patient becomes sleepy at this point. Are you feeling tired now Aaron?" Aaron replies, "Yes I am getting a little sleepy." Dr. Jaims says, "OK we can turn down the lights and let you get some rest."

The doctors leave the room and dim down the lights. They return to Dr. Blake's office where they have some monitors set up to see a screen that is mostly dark with the lights down, a monitor with a night vision lens, and a monitor with a thermal image to pick up any hot spots on Aaron's body. There is also a monitor with his vital signs. These are all being recorded by Dr. Jaim's computer for future analysis. The glasses that Aaron is wearing also calculate the size of his pupils. As his brain processes the image displayed his pupil is enlarged rapidly to take in more of the image. There is a counter on the lower left of this recording that displays the diameter in hundredths of millimeters. Dr. Jaims walks to his computer and says, "Let's go back in time and see how Aaron's patterns are on the imagery flash test." All four of the screens are reversed back to when Aaron first started the test. When Dr. Jaims presses play the videos are all synced and play in the same frame. Dr. Jaims watches the first couple slides and continues, "Based on my experience, it seems like his pupils are dilating less than a normal person. That means his mind or imagination fills the gaps from previous recall of the image. In other words, he uses less of his vision to tell his mind the story and relies more on his eidetic recall to paint the picture. See here? Just as I suspected it would happen. When we flash to the backside of the woman his eyes dilate more rapidly because he must use more of the image to get his answer to the slide. Dr. Blake chimes in here, "What does this mean for Aaron and our future testing?" Dr. Jaims answers, "The way your mind uses sight is a funny thing. Aaron's mind is more apt to rely on his memory than the average person. So, when you told me he could reconstruct a game of chess after only seeing the game for the first time for 30 seconds. This proves the theory. Some people can just recall items easier than others. Some people can recall license plates they had only seen and not memorized. I bet if I asked Aaron for your license plate number, he could recite it without hesitation.

Heck with Aaron's mind we could probably show him a picture of his bicycle for 15 seconds, take it away and then ask him how many spokes hold together his wheels. We could get a fairly accurate answer I bet. Given this, I am excited to do further testing tonight and into the morning. Under a slight hypnosis we can dive deeper into those long-term memories he has in the vault. This will help us to see back to when his mom was still alive. Dr. Blake asks, "Is it possible to dive too deep into the memory vault?" Dr. Jaims says, "Yes and no. Some people have an emotional connection to memories. Usually someone with an eidetic memory is less connected emotionally because their images are stored differently, but you never can tell until you get into that vault."

Dr. Blake jumps in and says, "Sorry to change the subject but I must call Christie every hour with an update. She told me it doesn't matter how late it is; I must call." Dr. Jaims presses LIVE on the monitor and the video jumps to a LIVE feed of Aaron. Dr. Jaims says, "OK, I will start a fresh pot of coffee in the break room and continue to monitor Aaron. It looks as if he is in the first stages of sleep right now. Possibly in an hour we can jump in and try a test."

Dr. Blake goes back to a private room, and he decides to call Det. Roberts first. "Roberts." The detective answers just as he is just getting back from dinner with his fiancé. "Detective Roberts, this is Dr. Blake. I wanted to get you an update on our progress with Aaron the first night. We have administered the first test, and it is very promising to Dr. Jaims. Aaron is showing signs of memory recall just as we suspected. We will continue with the tests throughout the night, but Dr. Jaims has said the deeper evaluation of his early memories will not happen until tomorrow night." Det. Roberts says, "OK well if you get any evidence that Aaron can remember back to that time, I would like to be there to hear what he has to say. Are you recording these next couple days for use later?" Dr. Blake answers, "Yes we are recording on 4 monitors, and we will not miss anything the next couple nights." Det. Roberts says, "Well I have some specific questions I would like you guys to ask if that is OK. I can drop off a list of questions tomorrow with your secretary. I am assuming you will not be in the office tomorrow since you are testing all night, correct?" Dr. Blake answers, "Yes we are not coming back until the evening, but Mrs. Kawley will be here to answer phones and to do some paperwork." Det. Roberts says, "OK and good luck with the testing tonight and look for my list tomorrow. Bye."

Dr. Blake hangs up and dials Christie Flint. Christie answers, "Dr. Blake, it is about time you called me. I have been pacing this house like a momma bear with a lost cub." Dr. Blake apologizes, "Sorry Christie, we have been busy with the first rounds of testing. Aaron is doing great. He is sleeping now and will be in a deeper sleep in the coming hour. We have covered some ground in the first rounds of testing and Aaron is being a real trooper." Christie asks, "Will you be disrupting his sleep a lot tonight? If you must do this again tomorrow, then he will need his sleep." Dr. Blake says, "We will give him an extra hour of sleep before we bring him back to you tomorrow. Hopefully that will make up for it. You have been keeping him on the strict 10-hour sleep regimen, and we plan to make sure he has 10 hours of sleep tonight. Tomorrow will be the same." Christie jumps in, "If Aaron asks for anything, anything at all, and it is something I can help with, just reach out and let me know. Anytime of night, you just give me a call and I will rush it over." Dr. Blake says, "OK, Christie we will do that." Christie always has to say the last word, so she jumps in and says, "OK now you call me again soon now, you hear me.

It is 10pm now so you better call me by midnight!"
Dr. Blake says, "I will, midnight it is."

Dr. Blake hangs up and walks back to his office where the monitors are and doesn't see Dr. Jaims in there. He goes over to the monitors to check on Aaron's vitals and movement. He looks in on the room and sees Dr. Jaims sitting next to Aaron in the side chair next to the bed. It looks like he is whispering to Aaron. The microphone isn't quite picking up exactly what he is saying. So, Dr. Blake decides to walk over and into the exam room where Aaron is sleeping. When he walks in, Dr. Jaims puts his index finger to his lips as if to tell Dr. Blake to be quiet, and then he points his finger toward the sky in a "wait a minute" gesture. Dr. Blake stops where he is and listens to what Dr. Jaims is whispering to Aaron, who is subconsciously sleeping. Dr. Jaims says, "Aaron we are going to be testing your memory tonight. We would like your full cooperation. Please let us do our work to keep you comfortable and we need you to just melt down into the couch. You will be one with the couch and the blanket will protect you from any memories you have been guarded from in the past. We will be seeking a full flow of open knowledge of the past. We will be back in a few minutes to get started. Please keep your position within the couch and continue to melt down into the cushions. It will be a safe place for your mind and soul." He stands up and walks toward Dr. Blake slowly whispering, "Let's go." And he points out of the room to the hallway. Once they are in the hallway Dr. Jaims says, "Let's go see if that coffee is done, it's gonna be a long night." They both walk to the back and into the break room.

Dr. Jaims grabs a coffee cup and begins pouring. Dr. Blake says, "What is the plan from here?" Dr. Jaims sighs and says, "Well in about 20 minutes I would like to see what we can do with the information you got out of Melvin. I reviewed the recording you sent me last week and made some notes for tonight. Do you have those photo albums from Christie?" Dr. Blake says, "Yes, they are in my office. Dr. Jaims says, "Good. I am not sure if she told you, but I had Mrs. Kawley put them on slides for the projector. I gave her some instructions on which ones I needed in color and which ones we needed black and white." After a pause of silence to take a sip of coffee Dr. Jaims continues, "If we can get him talking about those early years the rest will fall like dominoes." Dr. Blake says, "What do you mean, *the rest*?" Dr. Jaims says, "Well we could get to the bottom of what happened the day his mother died. I believe that is what has been holding him back in your treatments. He has been subconsciously closing off that part of his memory." Dr. Blake says, "OK then. Let me get the photo albums and the slides we had made, and my notes from that day with Mel at the prison. I will help you come up with a string of questions for Aaron. We can also get the slides in order of discussion."

Dr. Blake walks to his office and grabs his notebook. While he was there his phone rang. He answers, "Dr. Blake here." The voice on the other end says, "Hey Dr. Blake, it is Detective Roberts. Can you spare a minute? I've talked with the DA, and he wants you guys to ask about blood or anything that would provide DNA evidence. Also, he said to ask about tattoos and scars, or anything that will jump out as identifiers that would help us in a conviction of a person if it were steered in a direction other than Melvin Casey as the killer. We need something that will solidify a re-trial with new evidence." Dr. Blake says, "OK, we will try our best." Det. Roberts says, "OK, good luck, and call me if you discover anything new. Goodnight." Dr. Blake hangs up the phone and walks into the break room where Dr. Jaims is rinsing out his coffee cup. They both sit at the table and begin to brainstorm the next line of questioning. The table is filled with photo albums, photo slides, a projector, notebooks, coffee cups and coffee cake. Dr. Jaims looked at Dr. Blake and said, "It will be a long night and the work begins now."

Chapter 18

Overnight Test - Session 2

Dr. Blake grabs the carousel of slides and walks into the room where Aaron is sleeping. He goes to the projector and removes the slides from Aaron's last test, and he puts the carousel in with the slides from the pictures he received from Christie. He turns on the projector and it starts to warm up. While he is doing that Dr. Jaims walks over to the seat near Aaron. Aaron is in a deep sleep and Dr. Jaims feels bad because he must wake him up. He needs to wake him up slowly, so he begins whispering to Aaron. Dr. Jaims whispers, "Aaron, I'm not sure if you can hear me but we are going to begin the next set of tests. We will be leaving the lights down low, and we will use the projector again. The projector contains slides that depict major events from your life as a toddler. We have received some slides from your Aunt Christie. They will show your 2nd birthday, and your baptism in Boston. We have a few slides from a car accident you were involved in, and we have some photos from a time you visited your grandmother in the hospital. We also have some photos of your house from when you grew up and when your mother was around the house."

At this point, Dr. Jaims puts his hand on Aaron's shoulder. He does not shake him or push him at all; he just puts his hand on his shoulder in hopes that the warmth will wake him up. Aaron is laying there with his pupil detection glasses still on. He has a blanket covering up to his waist and he has the monitor still stuck to his chest and back. He also has a mini suction cup connected to his right temple. Dr. Jaims begins to talk a bit louder to Aaron now. Aaron begins to move his shoulders a bit and turn his position slightly toward Dr. Jaims. Dr. Jaims tells Aaron, "Are you comfortable in your position, currently?" Without opening his eyes Aaron shakes his head yes and moves his shoulders slightly. Dr. Jaims pushes the button on the slide projector remote to reveal the first photo. It shows Aaron sitting in the lap of his grandmother Anna. Dr. Jaims asks Aaron, "Hey bud, let's open our eyes and take a look at the slide on the ceiling." Aaron remains silent and does not move for almost a full minute.

At this time, Dr. Blake decides to go watch the monitors in his office. One of the monitors is recording the slides that are shown on the ceiling. Dr. Blake can see and hear everything in the room. He is happy that they decided to put a microphone on Dr. Jaims to pick up his soft hypnotic voice. Dr. Jaims asks Aaron again without touching him, "Aaron, please open your eyes and take a look at the slide on the ceiling." Aaron makes some movement again on his shoulders and head, but he does not open his eyes. Before he comes to rest Dr. Jaims repeats himself and says, "Aaron. Can you hear me, Aaron?" Aaron shakes his head yes. Dr. Jaims asks him again, "Please open your eyes and take a look at the ceiling." This time Aaron opens his eyes very slowly. On the monitors Dr. Blake can see his pupil dilation monitor spike to 90%. The glasses that Aaron is wearing emit a very faint green light. The green light is almost undetectable by Aaron, but it lights up the area around his eyes and face just enough for the night vision camera installed in the glasses to see his pupil. When Aaron sees the photo on the ceiling, he instantly whispers, in a sleepy voice, "Nana." Dr. Blake can remember when Aaron had told him that he called his grandmother Nana because it was so close to the name Anna. When he was young, he would always try to say Anna, but it would come out Nana, so the name stuck with him. In this photo, Anna is sitting in a lawn chair next to the pool and a table filled with presents and a purple Barney birthday cake. Dr. Jaims asks Aaron, "Do you remember your 2nd birthday?" Aaron shakes his head yes while keeping his eyes closed. Dr. Jaims asks Aaron, "Do you remember a clown from this day?" Aaron says, "Yes. He fell in the pool." Dr. Jaims asks Aaron, "Do you recall the color of the shoes the clown was wearing." Aaron answers, "No." Dr. Jaims takes the remote and pushes the button to advance to the next slide. This shows the clown from the waist up in black and white. Dr. Jaims asks Aaron to look at the slide on the ceiling. Aaron opens his eyes and sees the Clown. Dr. Jaims asks him again, "Do you remember what color his shoes are now?" Aaron continues to look at the clown photo and says, "Blue."

Dr. Blake has noticed in the office that Aaron's pupils have dropped to 73% dilated. Dr. Jaims asks Aaron, "Do you know what the clown is holding below his waist in this photo, where it is not revealed?" Aaron thinks for a minute and then closes his eyes. During this time, Dr. Blake noticed that his pupils dropped below 50% dilated before he shut his eyes. Aaron, with his eyes closed and with being half asleep, answers, "Barney." Dr. Jaims pushes the button on the remote to reveal the full photo in color. It shows a clown in a red jumpsuit with blue shoes and a purple Barney balloon animal. Dr. Jaims says to Aaron, "Take a look at the slide projected on the ceiling now." Aaron opens his eyes and sees the clown in color. Dr. Jaims says, "You were correct with your answers. Nice work." Dr. Jaims tells Aaron, "I will be right back." Aaron goes back to sleep while Dr. Jaims quietly leaves the room. He goes into Dr. Blake's control room to check the monitors. Dr. Blake gives him a rundown of what happened with the pupil monitor. Dr. Blake says, "When Aaron looked at the photo of the clown in color to see if his answers were correct his eyes were dilated at 93%. But when you asked about the blue shoes his pupils were at less than 50%." Dr. Jaims says, "This is, as I expected. Like before, he is using his imagination more than his eyes to remember the memory." Dr. Jaims adjusts the microphone on his collar and says, "Now, I'm going to go over the rest of the slides."

Dr. Jaims walks through and back into the exam room. He sits back down next to Aaron and once again puts his hand on his shoulder. He tells Aaron, "We will begin round 2." He pushes the button on the remote to reveal the next photo. He reveals a slide that shows Aaron, his mother, and father. Also in the photos is the priest that baptized him. Dr. Jaims asks Aaron, "Aaron, please look at the photo. Do you remember where this one was taken." Aaron opens his eyes to see them all standing on the front steps of the church and he says, "At the church." Dr. Jaims asks, "Do you know which church?" And Aaron replies, "In Boston." With Aaron's eyes still open he studies the photo. Dr. Jaims, without knowing the answer, asks Aaron, "Who was taking this photo?" Aaron says, "I don't remember." Dr. Jaims flips to the next slide to reveal Greg and Christie Flint holding Aaron. At this point, Aaron asks to see the last photo again. Dr. Jaims flips it back with the remote and Aaron says, "Now I remember it was Greg taking this photo." In his mind, Dr. Jaims realizes that showing the second photo of Greg and Christie holding Aaron at the church has sparked his memory, having known now that Greg and Christie were there. This in turn opens the memory banks to Aaron's brain. This places Greg at the scene. This is how photo elicitation works with most patients. Aaron is definitely coasting now. Dr. Jaims asks Aaron, "Now do you remember anything else from that day." Aaron says, "It was hot in the church and Father Gerald had an eye patch."

This line of questioning, not directly related to a photo is the route Dr. Jaims wants to go with the interviews now. Once Aaron gets a taste for a memory using photo elicitation there will be a breakthrough for many other memories to be revealed. Dr. Jaims hits the button on the remote to flip to the next slide that shows the inside of the church where Aaron was baptized. Dr. Jaims asks if this sparks any more memories of the day. Aaron says, "Yes. I remember running around the altar area on that green carpet. I also remember holding my mom's car keys. That carpet reminded me of green grass. Also, Father Gerald was telling me in his thick Boston accent, *Don't lose yah mahs cah keys or yah won't make the pahty afta this!* I thought it was funny." Dr. Jaims says, "Okay, let's move on." He pushes the button on the remote to show his mom and dad posing for a photo. His mom has a black eye, and his dad has a cast on his right arm, at the wrist. Dr. Jaims says, "Do you remember what caused this damage?" Aaron says, "No I don't remember." Dr. Jaims flips to the next slide, and it shows a Washington State Trooper Cruiser. Then Aaron says, "Yes, I remember. We rear-ended a State Trooper." Dr. Jaims says, "Yes. That is it. Do you remember anything else from that day?" Aaron says, "Yes. I remember Nana picked me up and we went for ice cream." Dr. Jaims says, "Do you remember an ambulance being at the accident scene?" Aaron must think for a second and he says, "Yes, I remember it came just as we were saying bye to Mom and Dad." Dr. Jaims asks, "Do you remember what color it was?" And

Aaron says, "Yes, it was mostly blue with white stripes." Dr. Jaims says, "Okay, I need you to think back. This was before you could read so I'm wondering if you can remember what it said on the side of the ambulance?" Aaron says, "I can remember some red letters on the side, but I have no idea what it said. I do remember there was a heartbeat symbol before and after the words." At that moment, Dr. Jaims hit the button on the remote to reveal a photo of an ambulance at a car crash scene. It was not the actual car crash that his Mom and Dad were involved in but he's hoping that the photo will spark a memory from Aaron's experience. The slide is filtered with an Amber color because Dr. Blake said that he had associated Ambulances with an Amber tone with his Synesthesia. Dr. Blake found the old flash cards that he used in Aaron's training when he was 4. The Ambulance card was an Amber color to help him make an association to the spelling of the word Ambulance to the Amber color. Anytime Aaron sees or hears an ambulance he has written in his journal that he would see a flash of amber colors in his mind. This was also listed in that hard file that Dr. Jaims had discovered after his first round of testing. After looking at the amber filtered Ambulance photo Aaron said, "Oh wait there was a silhouette of a pelican and now I remember it said Pelican Ambulance Service." Dr. Jaims says, "Good. Good work, Aaron. These are the small details we like to know that you can remember. This was at a time when you could not read, however the more we discussed a specific moment, the more you can remember. Also, with the help of photo elicitation, even though it is not the exact moment in time the smaller details that you remember turn into larger details. The heartbeat symbol led to the next part of the picture in your memory. With the introduction of the amber filter, it stimulates that part of your brain that remembers. We will let you sleep the rest of the night now and we can dive deeper into this tomorrow. We will talk more in the morning." Aaron says, "Okay, Dr. Jaims. Thank you and I'm excited for tomorrow."

At this time, Dr. Jaims turns off the projector and leaves the room. He begins to walk back to Dr. Blake's office to check on the monitors. Halfway down the hallway he can hear Dr. Blake talking to someone and he wonders who it is. He begins to walk a little slower, and quieter, to see if he can pick up on the conversation. That's when he hears the voice of Detective Jon Roberts. He is in shock that he is here because of the late hour. He turns the corner and walks into the room and says, "Detective Roberts, hello and it's nice to see you at such a late hour." He extends his hand to shake with Dr. Jaims. Detective Roberts says, "I was just watching you on the monitors with Dr. Blake and I am very impressed with your work." Dr. Jaims says, "Yes, now that we know he has synesthesia we can add that as a mechanism to drill into those deeper memories." Det. Roberts says, "Synesthesia? I have never heard of that." Dr. Blake answers, "This is another additional gift I discovered in Aaron at an early age." Dr. Jaims jokingly says, "Discovered or embedded? HA HA." Det. Roberts says, "Well whatever you guys are doing it seems to be working. I'm excited to see what tomorrow will bring, and if we can tap into those memories Aaron has from the night of his mother's murder. If you don't mind, I would like to be here for that tomorrow?" Dr. Jaims looks at Dr. Blake and says, "I don't see why not." Detective Roberts says, "Okay then. I'm going to hit the road and get some sleep. You guys compile some of the information from tonight and we'll see you in the morning." Dr. Jaims frowns and says, "You're coming back again in the morning?" This is where Dr. Blake joins in and says, "Yes, he's coming back at 10 a.m. to give us some more specific questions about the evening that Jackie was killed." Detective Roberts says, "Yes, Bryce has some specific questions he wants you guys to ask regarding the day Jackie was murdered. I left them back at the police station, so I'll have to bring them in the morning." Detective Roberts heads out of the office, and Dr. Jaims looks over a Dr. Blake and says, "Boy, this is really getting intense." Dr. Blake says, "I was watching the monitors while you talked to Aaron and it's very interesting to see how he reacts to many of the questions and photographs that you put in front of him. The pupil dilation monitor is very interesting to me, and you may have to look at it and decipher some of his reactions for me. I need to have a better understanding of it tomorrow when we dig deeper with Aaron." Dr. Jaims looks to end the night and says, "Yes, I would like to just get some rest and maybe get up early around 7 a.m. to get a few hours of research in on our work today before Detective Roberts stops by. We will need to wake Aaron around 9:30, that will put him at the 10-hour mark for sleep. This will keep him in a good disposition for tomorrow's work." Both men agree to call it a night. Dr. Blake says, "I will go check that the doors are locked and if you want there is a pull-out couch in the spare office that you can use. I will stay here in the office on my futon. It also folds down." Dr. Jaims says, "That sounds good. See you in the morning."

Chapter 19

Ben Henke & the 88th St. Diner

Detective Roberts walks into the old 88th St. Diner at around 12 a.m. He tells the hostess, "There will be two." She escorts him to a booth in the corner of the Diner. This is one of those old Diners you always see in the movies with the stainless-steel bar and stools that are fastened to the floor, with some tables in the middle and booths around the outside perimeter. It had a checkered floor, and the smell of bacon and eggs started for the 2nd shifters that worked 3 to 11. There were three guys sitting at the counter. They looked like they had just gotten off from the paper mill down the street. The booth that Detective Roberts was sitting in was far enough away from the counter so that nobody would hear the conversation that he would have with Ben Henke, the prior District Attorney.

Just then, Detective Roberts looked up and saw Ben walking in. He was wearing a khaki-colored trench coat and a gray hat. This is typical clothing for a man in his early 60's in the Seattle area when it rains. Ben walked in and saw Detective Roberts sitting down so he went straight to the booth. The waitress was following him up and before he could even sit down, she asked, "Can I get you gentlemen something to drink?" They both asked for coffee, and she went her way to get it started. Ben looked over at Detective Roberts and extended his hand for a handshake and said, "It's been a few months, old friend." Detective Roberts pressed his lips, gave a little nod and shook his hand. Detective Roberts begins by saying, "Ben we've got trouble brewing in the DA office. I wanted to come tell you in person and this seemed like the best place." Ben looked to see if anyone was close and said, "Oh yeah, what's going on?" Detective Roberts said, "Well, the Melvin Casey files are being looked at currently. Bryce, the new DA, is a pretty smart guy and he's digging pretty deep. Do you remember Mel's son?" Ben says, "Yes, I remember his son. What was he like, three or four when we were at trial?" Detective Roberts says, "Yes. He's 11 years old now and he has some sort of photographic memory. He's been working with a couple doctors. Or as you always called them, "shrinks." They think they can get him to remember what happened to Jackie. Remember the boy was in the house when it happened?" Just then, the waitress came over with their coffees and she asked if they were ready to order. Detective Roberts looks up at her and says, "Can you give us a few more minutes?" She says, "Yes, just wave me over when you guys are ready." She goes back to work at the counter. Ben looks over at Detective Roberts and laughs. He says, "There is no way that kid will remember what happened. He was only like 3 years old. And even if he does there's no way any jury will believe that he can remember back ten years." Detective Roberts looks down in his coffee cup and says, "This boy is pretty good. I've seen him in action and it's unbelievable. They have a doctor from San Francisco working with him. His name is Dr. Brian Jaims. He works with gifted children in court cases. When you get home, search for him on the internet. He's done some pretty amazing things that have held up in court. Ben says, "Okay, let's say they get something out of this kid? How will that connect either of us?" Detective Roberts looks up from his coffee to Ben Henke and says, "I am sure it will be all downhill from there. Building a case would not be that hard, especially if the right people say the right things." At that point, Ben points his finger to the table and says while gritting his teeth, "That's why you're still in the position you're in today. Work this thing and keep it from going south. DO what you have to DO to manipulate the system!" As he starts to get up from the booth he says, "Call me if you need some muscle. I still have a few connections down south."

Ben Henke walks to the door and heads out to his car. Just then the waitress comes up to the table and asks, "Is he coming back?" Detective Roberts says, "I don't think he is. I'll just go ahead and order. Can you get me a piece of that chocolate silk pie in the carousel?" The waitress says, "Sure Hun, I'll bring it right over." Detective Roberts looked out to Ben Henke's car and he can see that he got in and was now on his cell phone. At this point, the waitress brings over that piece of pie and tells him, "Enjoy. It was the last piece in the whole diner."

Ben gets back to his car and pulls out a cell

phone. He flips it open and looks up a guy named George Gallapolos. He was the guy he originally hired to get rid of Mel. He dials the phone and as soon as George answers he says in his raspy mob style voice, "Do you know what time it is? What are you calling me for, anyway." Ben looks down at the clock in his car and says, "Oh, I'm sorry. I forgot it's past midnight. Hey, we have a problem here. Detective Roberts just talked to me at 88th Street Diner. He told me Bryce is looking into the Melvin Casey files." George jumps in and says, "Who the hell is Bryce?" Ben says, "He's a new DA. He has some new evidence in the case. That kid that was home when you were there, remember him? He is 11 years old now and he has a photographic fucking memory. We've got to do something about this kid man. Detective Roberts is telling me he's gifted, and these Shrinks are going to get him to remember everything. I don't know if we can just scare him or what we got to do but the kid can't talk. Do you have any ideas?" George grumbles and says, "I'm not the brains here. Just tell me what to do and I'll do it. I'm not going back to jail over something that was 10 years ago. And you better have another paycheck for me on this one. Cuz I ain't doing it for free!" Ben says, "Don't worry about it. I got you covered, just wait for my call. I'll let you know what to do. Let me check out this kid. I'll find out his routine. We'll see if we can grab him and scare the shit out of him."

All of a sudden, the passenger side door of Henke's car opens. It's Detective Roberts. He sits down in the seat and shuts the door. He says, "Hey, who are you talkin' to? Is that George?" Ben says, "Yes, it's George. What the hell do you want?" Detective Roberts says, "I want to know what you guys are planning. You better not be working to hurt this kid." Ben says, "Don't worry about the angles we are working. You just find out a way to keep this kid quiet. We'll work on Plan B. George, I'll call you back tomorrow night with a plan."   He flips closed the cell phone and looks over at Detective Roberts and says, "Alright get the fuck out of my car. I'm getting out of here. Remember, keep the kid quiet! Put those quacks on a wild-goose chase or something. I don't know, figure something out." Detective Roberts opens the door and gets out of the car. Ben Henke drives away in a hurry. Detective Roberts goes over to his car and heads home.

Chapter 20

Bryce's Questions

7 a.m. comes fast. Dr. Jaims wakes up to his alarm. He rolls over to hit the snooze and he decides to sit up and put his glasses on. Then he grabs his glass of water and takes a swig. He slept in his clothes last night. He decides to walk over to the lunchroom and start a pot of coffee before he grabs some fresh clothes. The bathroom at the far back of the office has a corner shower. That shower is all he can think about as he makes the coffee. Once he has the coffee on. He goes back to his room and looks into his suitcase for fresh clothes. At this point, the snooze goes off on his phone. He walks over to the bedside table and shuts it off. He grabs his clothes, and he walks them to the back bathroom, where he's going to take a shower. He turns on the hot water, sets his clothes on the counter, and looks at himself in the mirror.

After a few minutes, he leaves the bathroom to go grab a cup of coffee. When he gets in there, he sees Dr. Blake taking the first cup. Dr. Blake turns around with a big grin on his face, and a full cup of coffee. Dr. Jaims says, "Is my coffee really that good or did you just wake up happy this morning?" Dr. Blake is swallowing his second sip of coffee and then he is speechless. Dr. Jaims says,

"What's going on Thom?" Dr. Blake reaches into his chest pocket and pulls out a photo. He says, "I found this photo in the album that I got from Christie. I think it's going to help today." He hands it over to Dr. Jaims, and when he looks at the photo his jaw drops. It is a photo of Jackie standing in the hallway above the stairs where she was killed. Dr. Jaims says, "Where'd you find this? It was not in the copy's you guys sent me and I did not see this in the album when I looked through them last night." Dr. Blake says, "Yeah, it was in the back page, and it was buried under about three other pictures." Dr. Jaims says, "Well, that's good. We'll definitely get some use out of this one." Dr. Blake says, "Before you got up, we got a phone call from Detective Roberts. He's already on his way." Dr. Jaims says, "I'm going to jump in the shower quickly, and put on some fresh clothes. Is Aaron still sleeping?" Dr. Blake says, "Yeah, last I looked he was still sleeping. Are we still leaving him to sleep until 9:30?" Dr. Jaims says, "Yes, have you talked to Christie yet?" Dr. Blake laughs and says, "Yes. I called her with the plan last night before we went to bed. She was glad we were finished for the night."

Dr. Jaims took his cup of coffee and went back to the bathroom. He left the photo on the table in the break room and Doctor Blake grabbed it up. He put it back in his chest pocket. Just then he heard the buzzer from the front desk. That's probably Detective Roberts he thought to himself. He walked up front to see that it was Detective

Roberts in his street clothes. He says, "Good morning, Detective Roberts. It must be a casual Saturday, huh?" Detective Roberts says "Yeah, I'm off duty today. I've got the list of questions from Bryce." Dr. Blake says, "Okay, come back to the break room with me. We'll grab a cup of coffee." Detective Roberts says, "That sounds great." He followed him back to the lunchroom. As Dr. Blake poured him a cup of coffee Detective Roberts says, "That was pretty impressive what you guys pulled off last night? Hopefully tonight goes the same." Dr. Blake says, "I'm sure it will be similar. Right now, we have Aaron sleeping until 9:30. That will give him 10 hours of sleep and that's what he is used to getting. After that, he can go home and enjoy this beautiful day with his friends. Then he'll be back here around 8 p.m. to begin the next phase of testing." Detective Roberts handed him the list and said, "Take a look and let me know what you think." Dr. Blake looked at the questions and he was very puzzled. He told Detective Roberts, "Normally in these situations we would like to let Aaron run the show. He should drive the conversation. We must keep the questions to a minimum." Detective Roberts says, "Well, if you guys get to a point where you've hit a wall, we would like you to ask these specific questions. Or at least they can be used as a guide for his direction so we can get more info on what happened the day of Jackie's murder." Dr. Blake decided to read a few out loud that he found to be a little disturbing. Dr. Blake says, "You want us to ask if he remembers seeing blood? And if he remembers seeing his mom pushed down the stairs? And, if he can remember who it was, and who grabs his mother at the top of the steps?" Detective Roberts says, "What? Yeah, we need him to pretty much say it out loud after a direct line of questioning. It must be framed in a way that we can prosecute someone. If he just offers the information, under an unconscious state the jury may not believe or understand how he could remember the act if he is partially asleep." Dr. Blake says, "Okay. Well, I understand that. But it's just hard for us to ask these questions. Especially when he's basically still a kid. I mean it's like walking up to a child and saying, "Hey kid, who killed your mom?"

At this point. Dr. Jaims walks into the room with his empty coffee cup and wet hair. Dr. Jaims says, "Hey guys. I need some more coffee." Detective Roberts looks over and says, "Good morning, Dr. Jaims. How did you sleep last night?" Dr. Jaims says, "I slept pretty good. I didn't wake up at all, not even for a bathroom break. It must be this damp air in Seattle." Detective Roberts laughs and says, "Yeah, it's like sleeping next to a humidifier when you're sick." Dr. Blake says, "You're going to have to see these questions Detective Roberts brought to us. Most of them are fine, but there's a few that cross the line in my opinion." Dr. Jaims pours a cup of coffee and then he sits at the table and grabs the piece of paper with the questions on them. He says, "Yeah, this is not going to work. We can't straight up ask him these kinds of questions. He must walk himself into remembering what happened on his own." Detective Roberts says, "Well, a little push in a certain direction shouldn't hurt, right?" Dr. Jaims says, "I've never had luck with asking direct questions like this." Detective Roberts says, "Bryce would like him to answer these questions directly, for the jury to clearly understand." Dr. Jaims says, "Usually with this type of thing, I testify before we show the evidence. That way the jury will know how this technique works. And I explain what they should look for. I can also help you guys with selecting the jury. I will give you questions to ask them, so we don't get a lot of realists in the group. You almost have to believe in hypnotism and these sorts of things. We can turn non-believers, but some of them are pretty stern. So, you can weed those out of the jury pool." Detective Roberts says, "I will have Bryce call you guys today and you can discuss this jury stuff and how you will testify to the techniques. I'm sure he will not like it, but maybe he will go along with it."

Chapter 21

Greg Talks to Aaron

Doctor Blake pulls his car into the driveway at the Flint household. The garage door is open, and they can see Greg is working on his Chopper. Doctor Blake tells Aaron, "Good job last night. You did well. We'll do it again tonight. Now go have some fun today because you won't be a kid forever" Aaron said, "Okay. Thanks Doctor Blake, I'll see you later." Aaron gets out of the car and walks up to the garage.

Just as he gets in the garage, Greg says, "Hey Slugger, will you hand me that wrench right there?" and he points to the workbench. Aaron grabs the wrench and hands it to Greg. Greg says, "Hey, how was the night?" Aaron said, "It went well. At least that's what they tell me." Greg asks, "What kind of questions are they asking you?" Aaron says, "Oh, just about things from when Mom and Dad were around." Greg says, "Are you okay with telling them about the stuff?" Aaron says, "I guess I don't know what the big deal is." Greg says, "Well, did they ask you about when your mom died?" Aaron says, "No, not yet but I think they will tonight." Greg says, "Well you don't have to answer any of those questions if you don't want to, they're just looking for something to hook on you. Make sure you tell the truth and don't make up any stories just to keep them happy!" Aaron says,

"Okay, okay. I didn't know this bothered you so much." Greg says, "It doesn't. I just don't want to see you get hurt." Aaron says, "I'll be fine I've been waiting to talk about this for a long time, and Christie says it will be good for me." Greg says, "Yeah. Well, Christie doesn't know everything. She had a perfect life growing up, she's not like you or me." Greg's mom had died when he was 8 years old. So, he kind of felt like he knew what Aaron was going through. Greg's dad also was a truck driver, so he was on long trips all the time. He grew up around his grandmother most of the time. Aaron tells Greg, "I know if I get to a point where I don't want to talk anymore, I will just let them know." Greg says, "I think that's a good idea and it's even okay if you don't want to go tonight at all. I will back you up. Just remember don't make up any stories just to satisfy the doctors. Make sure you tell the truth. Hey, it may even help your dad who knows."

Greg decides to change the subject and tells Aaron, "Hey, Miley called this morning she wanted to know when you got back. I think she has something planned for you guys today. So go inside and give her a call." Aaron says, "Okay, great I'll give her a call right now. Where is Christie?" Greg says, "She went to the grocery store. She'll be right back." Aaron runs into the house and dials Miley's phone number. Miley answers the phone like she was sitting there waiting for him to call. She says, "Hey Aaron, will you have time to go with me down to Penny stream? I want to fish down there today."

Aaron says, "Sure, I'll meet you at your house in about 30 minutes and we can ride together on the bikes."

Chapter 22

Ben Visits Angie VanPatton

The next morning, Ben Henke crosses the bridge into Sacramento. He looks for the signs that say 57th Avenue. Once he gets to the exit, he pulls off and looks for 8th Street. Once he gets down the street, he sees a blue house with a white picket fence. He stops the car and walks up to the door. He rings the doorbell. A young woman answers the door and says, "Can I help you?" Then Henke says, "Yes, I'm looking for Angie VanPatton. Does she live here?" The girl yells behind her, "Mom, somebody's at the door for you." When Angie walks up, she sees that it is Ben Henke and she tells her daughter, "Thanks Hannah. I'll take it from here." She waits for Hannah to run upstairs back to her room, and she invites Ben into the house.

When they reach the kitchen, she asks if he wants a cup of coffee and he says, "No, this won't take long." He tells her, "You have to know why I'm here." She says, "Yes, I never wanted to see you again, but I always wondered if you would show up. And here you are." He says, "Okay, so you know WHAT I'm here about. Now let's concentrate on WHY I am here. They have new evidence in Mel's case, and I want to make sure that you're still on board with what you testified. We held up our side of the bargain with the 20 grand and we did not hurt Hannah. Please do not make us go back on that. If they come here asking questions, you must stick to the story. I've already spoken to George, and he has decided to stay in a hotel close by here for the next few weeks. Just remember he's only a phone call away. I am assuming they will want to talk to you again. Detective Roberts is still in the department, and he will try his best to keep them from coming to see you, but I can't make any promises. That's all I have for you, at this moment. He walks over to Angie close enough to whisper in her ear while clenching his jaw, "Remember…. George's close….. and stick to the story!" Then he walks out of the house and back to his car without another word. He drives back to Seattle knowing that Angie should be in check.

Chapter 23

Aaron Fishing with Miley

Aaron finishes putting away the groceries and he asks Christie, "Can I run down to the fishing hole with Miley?" Christie says, "Sure, just make sure you get home around 1 for lunch." Aaron grabs his hat and his play shoes and runs out to the garage to grab his tackle box and fishing pole. He grabs the pole and heads towards the Stream, along the way, he is crossing Miley's house, and he hears her yell from the garage, "Hey Aaron, wait up." Aaron turns his bike around and goes towards her garage. She has her tackle box and fishing pole and is getting onto her bike. Her bike has a basket on the front and her tackle box fits perfectly inside. It makes it easier for her to ride. She sets her fishing pole across her handlebars and begins to ride. She says, "Hey, I found a shortcut the other day, follow me." Just then she turns into the yard between the Holloway house and Mr. Matthew's driveway. This makes for a faster route onto Oak Street, that's when she turns right and heads towards the Stream. Once she gets to the field, you can see a path from four wheelers that take the shortcut also. She runs down the path and it goes straight toward where they like to fish. Once they cut across the tree line it follows down to a nice open spot with a beach-like feel with nice brown sand and an easy spot to put down their bikes and tackle boxes.

They both start to get their fishing poles ready. Miley says, "Hey, I brought a couple hot dogs. I thought they would be perfect bait." She breaks off the piece and throws it at Aaron, but he isn't ready. It bounced off his shoulder and onto the ground. Aaron says, "Hey, I'm going to smell like hot dogs now." She laughs and says, "Just put it on your hook and let's go." They both got it set on their hooks, and they threw it into the water. Miley looks over at Aaron and says, "How was your night?" Aaron says, "It wasn't too bad. They have some cool gadgets that I get to use." Miley says, "Oh yeah, like what?" Aaron says, "Well, they have these cool glasses that I must wear. They have a green light that shines on my eyes. I can't really tell that the light is on, but they can see my pupil as it dilates. They can tell if I'm looking at the picture or imagining the memory." Miley says, "Wow this Doctor Jaims is pretty good. How did he come up with that idea?" Aaron says, "I don't know but it seems to work well. Dr. Jaims says my eye is only dilated if the photo doesn't match my memory so most of the time my eyes dilated less than 50%." Miley starts to laugh and says, "So does that mean you have a blind memory?" Aaron starts to laugh, and he says, "I guess so. I probably remember things better with my eyes closed." Just then Miley's fishing pole bends over, and she says, "Hey I got a fish!" She grabs her reel and starts bringing in the line and she says, "I think it's a big one." Aaron says, "I'll go grab my Stringer. If it's a keeper, we can put it on the line." She gets it up to the shore and sees that it's a bullhead. She says, "Oh boy, it's one of those squishy fish with the horns. I'm not touching that thing." She ends up hard on a pole and the hook comes right out of the fish's mouth and she kicks the fish back into the water. She says, "Go back to where you came from, you stinky fish." Aaron says, "Remember that time, that one stuck you right in the hand. We had to go home and get a Band-Aid because you were bleeding all over? She says, "I know. I'm not touching one of those things again in my life." She looks at her hook and says, "Man he took my hotdog." So, she goes back to her tackle box and rips off another piece of hot dog and puts it on a hook. She throws her line out about 90 degrees from where she was fishing out over to where she caught the bull head and says, "I'm not fishing over there anymore. I'm going to try this spot." As soon as her line got settled, she put her fishing pole on top of the twig and walked over to Aaron. She said, "What are they going to do with you tonight, is it the same thing they have been doing?" Aaron says, "Yeah, I think they're going to talk more about Mom and Dad this time. It will probably get a little more intense. I hope that I can remember what happened to my mom. I've been thinking about it more these days leading up to the therapy sessions with Dr. Jaims. I do remember playing upstairs that day when it happened. We had this cool toy room, and I had all my army guys out, that is all I really remember. It was the room that I sleep in now."

Just then, they heard a dog barking in the woods on the other side of the stream. Miley said, "Hey, do you hear that dog? Aaron said, "Yes, I can hear it. It sounds like a small puppy." Miley says, "Yeah, let's go check it out." They both begin to reel in their fishing poles, and they set them down next to their bikes. They run to the bridge just down the stream. Miley is the first to start running towards the bridge and Aaron follows. They continue to hear the dog barking, and it sounds like he's getting closer to the bridge. Once they reach the bridge, they go across Penny Stream and get to the other side, once on the other side there's a lot more trees on that side of the bridge and they start to run into the thick of the woods. They continue to hear the dogs bark get closer and Miley says, "Do you think it's over there?" And Aaron says, "Yes, keep going." They get a bit closer, and Miley is still in the lead. She runs up ahead and she turns back to see where Aaron is, and she trips on a root. She falls to the ground and scrapes her knee on one of the branches from another tree that's fallen to the ground. Aaron yells, "Are you OK?" And Miley says, "Yeah, I think I'll be alright." She rolls over and grabs onto her knee. Aaron finally catches up and gets close to her. He says, "Let me take a look at your knee." That's when they continue to hear the dog barking, and it gets closer. That's when Miley turns her head back towards the path and yells, "Here boy, here boy, over here!" Aaron says, "Don't worry about the dog. Let me see your knee." She pulls her hand away and there's some blood. It looks like she got a pretty good raspberry.

Aaron takes a handkerchief out of his pocket and hands it to Miley. He says, "Put this on there and I will get some water from the stream to wipe it down." Aaron gets in close to her knee and he says, "Pull it off for a second." She pulls the handkerchief away from her knee. It is clean now and Aaron begins to blow on it to help the blood clot. Aaron says, "Does that hurt?" Miley says, "No, that doesn't hurt but if you touch it, that will hurt." Aaron blows on her knee again and it looks like the bleeding has stopped.

Aaron stands up and holds out his hand to help her up. Once he pulls her up onto her feet she gives him a kiss on the cheek. Aaron says, "Hey, what is that for?" Miley says, "Well, for helping me. My knee feels better now. Thank you." Just then, Miley leaned in closer to give Aaron a kiss on the lips. That's when they heard barking very close. A beagle puppy jumps out from the bushes onto Aaron's leg. Then Miley says, "Oh my gosh, it's Ringo!" Aaron says, "Who the heck is Ringo?" Miley says, "That's Mr. Matthews new puppy. Mr. Matthews really likes the Beatles, and I told him he should name his puppy Ringo after Ringo Starr." Aaron says, "Who the heck is Ringo Starr?" And Miley says, "He's the drummer from The Beatles dummy. What, have you been living under a rock with your super memory?" Aaron says, "Well no but I guess I've never looked into Beatles trivia." Miley says, "We need to get Ringo back to Mr. Matthews. He's probably worried sick." Just then Ringo ran up the bank and into some brush. They left the main path and followed Ringo so they could catch him. Miley yelled, "Ringo, come back here!" as she led the way up into the brush. They climbed up and over the small hill and into some darker and thicker wooded area. Once they crossed into the next line of trees, they heard Ringo yipping off to the right. They followed the sound and then a large man grabbed Aaron's arm. Then Miley turned around to see Aaron being grabbed when he yelled, "Hey, let me go!" Just then, another man grabbed Miley and said, "Be quiet little girl and we won't hurt you?" The men are wearing work clothes, jeans, work boots, hoodies with the hoods up and bandanas over their nose and mouths. They are not identifiable at all.

They took Miley and Aaron into a small hunting shack and talked to them. They sat them down at a table and put Ringo in a cage. Miley said, "What are you going to do with Ringo?" And the man said, "This is not about the dog, he was just a distraction. We are here to talk to Aaron." Aaron said, "Why me?" The man said, "We need you to stay quiet about your mom's death. We know what you have been telling the Doctors. It needs to stop NOW!" Aaron says, "They have me under hypnosis. There is nothing I can do to stop them. I am unconscious when they ask me questions." The man says, "I don't care if they have you over a flame! Keep your mouth shut and we won't hurt your girlfriend." They grab Miley's arm harder, and she screams. With her free hand she hits the man's arm that has a hold of her, and she says, "Let me go, you creep!" The man just laughs. "Tell your boyfriend to stop talking to the doctors and cops and we will let you two go home." Miley says, "I am not telling him anything, you can't hurt us." The man grabs a pipe from the ground and hits the dog cage. Ringo yips loudly and the cage is dented badly. He said, "You will not tell anyone about this, and you will keep quiet, or we will be forced to hurt you and your families. Do you understand?" Aaron says, "Yes. Yes, we understand. I will tell them I don't feel good and that I cannot do the treatments anymore. Just let us go!" The man says, "This is what we want to hear, and we will be keeping an eye on you two!" Just then Miley grabs another pipe from the table and hits the man holding her right in the side of the face. He lets her go and says, "Why you little shit! Give me that pipe now!" He manages to grab her without being hit again and takes the pipe away. He looks over to his accomplice and says, "Let's go. Open the cage and they can take the dog back to that old man." He turns to Aaron and says, "Like we said, stop talking to the Doctors and we will leave your girlfriend and family alone!" Aaron says "OK!" They open the cage, and Ringo is curled up in the corner crying. He won't come out on his own. The man says, "Forget the dog, let's go!" They both left the shack in a hurry and Aaron and Miley were alone with the dog.

Miley came over to Aaron quickly and said, "Are you OK?" He said, "Yes. Are you? And she said, "Yes. I got that guy pretty good in the eye!"

Aaron said, "Let's get the dog and get out of here!"
They grabbed Ringo and put him on the leash that
was on the table. Miley had to pick him up
because he wouldn't walk out of there. They
walked back to their bikes on the beach and didn't
say a word. Before they left, Miley looked at Aaron
and said, "What should we do now?" Aaron said,
"Let's take back Ringo and just tell Mr. Matthew's
his dog was loose down by the beach. Then we will
go home and not say anything about the men. I
don't want to get anyone excited about what
happened. I will try to get out of my session
tonight." They both rode back, dropped off the
dog, and went home without another word.

Chapter 24

Aaron is Home from Fishing

Aaron rides his bike straight into the garage. He parks it next to the lawn mower off to the side of the garage and runs into the house. He runs past the kitchen and starts to head for his room. Before he gets too far, Christie says, "Wash your hands for lunch, it's almost ready." Aaron stops at the bathroom and washes his hands quickly. Aaron walks back towards the kitchen and Christie says, "Grab some plates and silverware so we can eat at the table together." Aaron grabs the items and walks over to the table and sets them in two places.

Shortly after Christie comes over with a bowl of tuna salad and bread along with some chips. They both make a sandwich and grab some chips. Christie says, "What do you want to drink?" Aaron says, "Just some water is fine, thanks." As Christie's filling up the water glasses she starts a new conversation, "How was the fishing?" Aaron says, "Not so good we caught a bullhead and that was it." Christie says, "Oh those things are gross. I hope you threw it back?" Aaron said, "Yeah Miley caught it and got it off the hook before we even had to touch it." Christie said, "Oh that's good. Anything else happened while you were out there? Aaron said, "Yeah, we heard a dog barking. Come to find out it was Ringo, Mr. Matthew's dog. He had gotten loose from his chain and was running around down by Penny stream." Christie said, "Were you able to catch him?" Aaron said, "Yes, Miley knows the dog well and he came right to her. We took him back to Mr. Matthew's House. That's why I'm back early." Aaron took one bite of a sandwich. He chewed it up, swallowed it and said, "I'm not really hungry. My stomach kind of hurts." Christie said, "When did this start? Are you feeling, okay? Aaron said, "While we were fishing, I started to feel kind of dizzy, but my stomach didn't hurt until I swallowed that first bite. Can I be excused from the table? I would like to lay down to see if that will help." Christie said, "Okay but don't fall asleep you have to work with Dr. Blake tonight again." Aaron said, "Okay."

Aaron walked upstairs to his bedroom. He paced back and forth a few times between his closet and his dresser, which was the length of his bedroom. He was trying to figure out what to tell Christie before she came up to check on him. He took off his shoes, changed his shirt, and put on some more comfortable shorts.

By the time Aaron lay back down after changing his clothes Christie was already knocking on his door. He said, "You can come in." Christie opens the door and says, "Hey Bud, you doing, okay? Aaron replies, "I still don't feel very good. Will you check my temperature? Christie put her hand to his forehead and said, "You feel okay to me. Let me grab a thermometer." Aaron thought to himself that there's no way I'm going to have a temperature. What else could I tell her? At that point she had already walked back into the room with the thermometer. She said, "Here, put this under your tongue for a few minutes we'll see what we get. Was the first time you felt sick down at the Stream?" Aaron mumbled and pointed to his mouth indicating that he couldn't talk at that moment. She laughed and said, "Okay I'll wait." A few moments passed and she said, "Okay, that's probably good." She grabbed the thermometer from his mouth and as she was reading the meter Aaron swallowed and said, "I didn't feel sick until I took that bite of lunch." She said, "Well you don't have a temperature. You're at 98.3, so you're fine. Maybe if you lay down, I can give Dr. Blake a call and see what he suggests for tonight." Aaron said, "Okay"

Christie walked out of Aaron's bedroom to put the thermometer away and then went downstairs to the phone in the kitchen. She dialed Dr. Blake's office and Mrs. Kawley answered the phone. She said, "Doctor Blake's office. How may I help you?" Christie replied, "Hello, this is Christie Flint. I'm calling to talk to Dr. Blake. Is he in the office?" Mrs. Kawley answered, "No he is out to lunch with Dr. Jaims. Would you like to leave a message?" Christie replied, "Sure, could you tell Dr. Blake that Aaron isn't feeling very well and to call me back as soon as possible." Mrs. Kawley said, "Sure. As soon as he is back, I will give him the message. Thank you." No less than three seconds after she hung up the phone Dr. Blake and Dr. Jaims came walking through the door. There was nobody in the waiting room, so Mrs. Kawley said, "I just got a call from Christie Flint, and she says that Aaron is not feeling well. You might want to give her a call back when you get to your office." Doctor Blake looked at Doctor Jaims and said, "Awe, this isn't good. Let's give her a quick call and see what's going on."

They get back to Dr. Blake's office and Dr. Jaims sits down in the big leather chair next to the window. Doctor Blake sits at his desk and dials Christie's number. When it begins to ring, he puts it on the speaker and sits back in his chair. Within two rings Christie answers the phone, "Flint residents." Dr. Blake starts, "Christie, it's Dr. Blake and Dr. Jaims. I have you on the speaker phone. What is going on with Aaron?" She said, "He went down to Penny Stream fishing, and he came back not feeling so well." Dr. Jaims steps towards the phone and says, "What are his symptoms?" She said, "He was dizzy down by the stream and when he came home, he took a bite of his lunch. He said his stomach was hurting and wanted to lay down." Dr. Jaims says, "He's not taking a nap right now, is he?" Christie said, "No, I told him not to fall asleep but that he could lay down for a little bit." Dr. Jaims says, "Good, don't let him sleep but he can rest." Christie says, "If it gets worse can we keep him home tonight and do the testing tomorrow night?" Doctor Blake says, "Dr. Jaims has a flight tomorrow night, I guess we could see if he could push his flight to Wednesday night?" Dr. Jaims says, "Let me call my office, and cancel Wednesday's appointments." Dr. Blake says, "You know what Christie? We have a good thing going. Is there any way that Dr. Jaims and I can swing by the house to see how Aaron's doing right now?" Christie says, "Sure, you guys can come by and check on him. We're not going anywhere." Dr. Blake says, "Great, we'll be right over." Dr. Blake picks up the receiver and sets it back down to close the phone call. He looks over at Dr. Jaims and says, "Nobody thought this was going to be easy." Dr. Jaims laughs and says, "Okay, let's go!"

As they walked out, Dr. Blake told Mrs. Kawley that she could lock up and head home. As they pull up to the house, they see Miley riding her bike towards the house also. They pull into the driveway, shut off the car and open their doors. Miley rides her bike right up to Dr. Blake. As Dr. Blake is getting out of the car he says, "Well hello Miley how are you?" Miley says, "I'm fine. I'm here to check on Aaron. He got sick while we were down by the Stream." Dr. Blake says, "Yeah, we heard the same. That's why we're here. We're going to check on Aaron too." Dr. Blake asks Miley, "What were you two doing down by the Stream?" Miley says, "We were fishing and then we heard a dog barking. It was Mr. Matthews dog, Ringo."

Just then Dr. Blake noticed that Mr. Matthews was walking his dog towards the house. Dr. Blake introduced himself and introduced Dr.

Jaims. Mr. Matthews replied, "Well hello. It's good to meet you. I'm Mr. Matthews from down the street. I'm here to talk to Aaron." The men looked at each other and Dr. Blake said, "Yes, so are we. Aaron is going to have a large group here to see him and he's not feeling well right now from what we've heard."

All four of them went to the door and rang the doorbell. Christie answered the door. To her disbelief, there were four people standing outside the door. She said, "Oh my gosh! What can I do for you all?" Dr. Blake started and said, "We're here to check on Aaron and I guess so is Miley and Mr. Matthews here with his dog." Christie said, "Well let me go grab Aaron. I think he's feeling okay walking around. Christie ran up the stairs and said, "Aaron there's a few people here for you." Aaron said, "I thought only Dr. Blake and Dr. Jaims were coming. Who else is here?" Christie said, "Well Miley is here and so is Mr. Matthews. He has a dog. I'm not sure what's going on there." Aaron looked up at the ceiling and then sat up quickly. Aaron quickly walked down the stairs to the front door. Dr. Blake was inside the entry and said, "Oh. Hey Aaron, you came down the steps quickly. Are you feeling better? Aaron sighed and said, "Well yeah, a little bit. Mr. Matthews is here too?" Mr. Matthews came into the door with Ringo. Mr. Matthews said, "Yes, I'm here. I need to talk to you, Aaron. Miley said you guys found Ringo down by the Stream. She won't tell me anything else. I had seen two men grab Ringo and walk away towards

151

the Stream. Do you know anything about these men?" Dr. Blake and Dr. Jaims looked at each other and then looked at Aaron. Aaron was drawing a blank. Dr. Blake said, "Do you know anything about this Aaron? Were there two men down by the stream with the dog?" Aaron said, "Well to tell you guys the truth, yes there were two men down at the Stream. They grabbed ahold of me and Miley." Mr. Matthews looked at Miley and said, "They did? Why didn't you tell me?" Miley said, "Because Aaron didn't want to tell anyone." Doctor Blake said, "We should probably call the police about this matter. Let me get a hold of Detective Roberts. He will know what to do."

Just then, Christie walked into the entryway from the kitchen, and she said, "What's going on in here?" Dr. Blake said, "I need to borrow your phone. I need to call Detective Roberts." Christie said, "Um, okay. Well, what's going on here." Mr. Matthews said, "Two men stole my dog and then they grabbed Aaron and Miley down by the Stream!" Christie said, "This is true, Aaron? Why didn't you tell me?" Aaron said, "I didn't want to scare you." Christie said, "And is this why you're not feeling well?" Aaron answered, "Yes." Christie quickly replies, "Okay. Well, when the detective gets here tell him the truth." Aaron says, "OK" Just then Dr. Blake came back into the entry and said, "Detective Roberts is on his way." Christie said, "Why don't we all wait outside for Detective Roberts to get here."

Once they all got onto the porch Christie asked if anyone wanted anything to drink while they waited. Everyone said they were okay. After a few more minutes Detective Roberts pulled up in his squad car. He got out and started to walk towards the house. He had on his uniform with his sunglasses and hat on. As he walked towards the group Ringo started to bark wildly. Mr. Matthews tried to calm him, and he said, "Ringo always goes crazy when the UPS guy comes to the house. I think it's the brown uniform." As Detective Roberts gets closer, he reached down to pet Ringo and he says, "Oh, hey boy, it's okay." Ringo tries to bite him, and he pulls back. He looks at Doctor Blake and says, "Most dogs don't like the uniform." Doctor Blake says, Detective Roberts we need to file a report." Detective Roberts says, "What about?" Doctor Blake says, "Well Mr. Matthews here, says two men took his dog and then the same two men grabbed Miley and Aaron down by the Stream." Dr. Jaims steps in and says, "Aaron, what did these men say to you?" Detective Roberts cuts off his answer and says, "I need to interrogate each of you separately to get the full story." At this point, Mr. Matthews' dog was still growling and barking. Det. Roberts said, "Mr. Matthews can you run your dog home?" I will come down to your place and get your statement after I finish here with the kids." Mr. Matthews agreed and took Ringo home.

Det. Roberts turned to the group and said, "OK, let's eliminate the baggage here. He looks at Dr. Blake and says, "Dr. Blake, were you and Dr.

Jaims here during any of this?" They both denied being involved and Det. Roberts told them they could leave or stick around. It was up to them. They both stayed and said they would like to wait to see what this is about. Christie turned to them both and said, "You guys can wait in the den, and I will put on a pot of coffee if you'd like?" Det. Roberts said, "Christie, before you start that coffee will you go down to Miley's house and get her parents. I need them here when I question her?" Christie agrees and starts her walk toward their house. Det. Roberts looks at the guys and says, "OK, let's take this into the house where we can get comfortable. It might take a while."

Chapter 25

The Police Report

Det. Roberts says, "Hi, you must be Mr. and Mrs. Sanders?" Her father steps up and asks, "Is she in trouble, officer?" Det. Roberts says, "No, of course not. I just need to know what she saw and heard during this event. You and your wife can listen in and oversee her part of the investigation." Miley walked over and said, "Hi Detective, I am Miley Sanders. It is nice to meet you." Det. Roberts said, "Likewise. Now please tell me everything that happened after you found the dog." Miley said, "Ringo, the dog's name is Ringo. Well, we found Ringo down by the water and he came right to me. As soon as we found the dog we were grabbed by the two men that Mr. Matthews described. They told Aaron not to talk to the doctors anymore and threatened to hurt me if he did." Miley's dad jumped in here, "Miley, who were these men?!" Miley looked over at him and said, "Dad, I don't know. I have never seen them in my life." Det. Roberts held up his hand and said, "Mr. Sanders we will find these men don't you worry." The Detective turned to Miley and said, "Is there anything you remember about these men that will help us find them." She said, "Yes, one of the guys should have a big old shiner because I jacked him in the head with a metal pipe. And the other guy had long black hair." Det. Roberts says, "Wow, that was brave of you. We need some bravery like that in the police force. Have you ever thought about being an officer some day?" Miley laughed and said, "No, but my uncle is a police officer in Chicago." Det. Roberts says, "Well you must get your courage from him, and I want to thank you for your statement. Here is my card. If you remember anything else just call that number on the card. I am going to talk with Aaron now."

Detective Roberts walks over to Aaron and Christie, and he says, "How about you Aaron? Do you have anything that you remember about these guys from the moment you found the dog? I guess the dog's name is Ringo. Who is the Beatles fan?" Aaron says, "Mr. Matthews loves the Beatles, I guess. Detective Roberts, these men were scary, and I don't want my family or friends to get hurt over this." Detective Roberts says, "Aaron, I have seen what you can do with your memory. Is there anything you can offer me that will help to capture these suspects? Did you hear any names? Or see any tattoos or features that will help to identify these men?" Aaron thinks for a minute and says, "Miley did bust one of the guys in the eye with a steel pipe, and the other man had some longer black hair from what I remember." Detective Roberts smiles and says, "Yeah, she told me that too. Brave girl you have there as a friend." Aaron said, "I don't really have anything else to offer at this time." Detective Roberts said, "Here is my card. If you remember anything else just give me a call. I am going down to meet with Mr. Matthews."

Dr. Blake walked into the kitchen and decided to speak up here with Det. Roberts still in the room. He said, "Det. Roberts, before you leave. I just want to tell you we can finish this tonight. Give Dr. Jaims and I one more night and we can close this case with Aaron's help." Dr. Blake looked over at Aaron and said, "Do you have the strength to give us one more night Aaron?" Aaron looked over at Christie and he said, "Yes I think I can give one more night to this as long as nobody gets hurt." Det. Roberts says, "We can put a unit out in front of Miley's house and your house for the night. I will also be at Dr. Blake's office for tonight's session." Aaron looks over at Christie again and says, "Pack my P.J.s, my toothbrush, and my pillow." He looks at Dr. Blake and Dr. Jaims and says, "Let's do this!" Det. Roberts said, "Let me go down and get Mr. Matthews' statement quickly and I will meet you all back at Dr. Blake's office."

Det. Roberts walks down to Mr. Matthews' house and knocks on the door. Mr. Matthews opens the door and Detective Roberts says, "Your turn, are you ready?" Detective Roberts asks him, "Just start off with telling me what happened from the beginning." Mr. Matthews can hear Ringo barking wildly from his laundry room and yells, "Ringo will you keep quiet!" Then he looks at Detective Roberts and says, "I went to let out Ringo and he ran right out the front door. Two men grabbed him, and they ran toward the area of the stream." Detective Roberts asked, "What did these men look like?" Mr. Matthews said, "They were both about your height, 6 foot tall or so and I didn't get to see much. One man had longer black hair, maybe shoulder length. That is really all I can say about them. They bent down and grabbed Ringo and then ran so all I saw were their backs. They were wearing work clothes, jeans, work boots, hoodies with the hoods up and bandanas on their nose and mouths. I don't think I could pick them out of a lineup." Det. Roberts gives him a card and gives him the same advice as Miley and Aaron. He says, "Call me if you remember anything more than that." Mr. Matthews said, "OK, I will. Thank you, Detective. Have a good night." Mr. Matthews shut the door and Det. Roberts was on his way.

Chapter 26

Overnight Two

Dr. Blake takes his keys and opens the office door to a dark lobby. He flips on the waiting room light and says, "Go ahead and get set up in the session room. I will grab the slides, and we can begin the usual 48 slide ceiling session to get you tired." Dr. Jaims, Christie, and Aaron all walk toward the back without even saying a word. Dr. Blake looked at his wristwatch and noted that it was already 7:48pm and they had a plan to start at 8pm so there was no time to waste. He walks back to his storage room and grabs the slide deck. Next to the slides is the photo he found the other day with Aaron's Mom at the top of the staircase. He looks out the window at the back of the room and says, "God, I hope this works." He snaps out of it and walks the slide deck back to the session room where Aaron is almost ready to get comfortable on the couch. He loads the slide deck into the photo carousel and turns the power on. He looks to Aaron and says, "I will let that warm up, I will be right back. Get comfortable, I will go see if Dr. Jaims is ready."

Dr. Blake walks back toward the break room wondering if they could get some coffee on, and he heard Dr. Jaims setting up the control room. He stops there and peaks his head in. Dr. Jaims speaks up first, "Hey, do you know where we put that photo of Aaron's mom on top of the stairs?" Dr. Blake says, "Yes, it was back in the storage room.

But I found the negative and made a slide for it."
Dr. Jaims smiles and says, "Great Thom! You are
always a step ahead of me and always have been."
Dr. Blake says, "OK Brian, next step for me is
starting the coffee, and I will make the dark roast
this time. We may have to pull an all-nighter." Dr.
Jaims laughs and says, "Someone is a step ahead of
you now and it is Christie, she is already making the
coffee." Dr. Blake says, "Oh good, I will go see if
she needs help."

While Dr. Blake goes to check on Christie,
Dr. Jaims turns on the microphone to the session
room and asks Aaron over the speakers, "Aaron,
are you comfortable yet? It's 8pm and I'd like to
start the slide deck." Dr. Jaims watches his
reaction on the live monitor and Aaron answers to
the speakers in the session room, "Yes, I am
ready." Dr. Jaims works the controls, and he dims
the lights and flips on the slide carousel. He pushes
play on the CD player, and they hear a chime and
picture descriptions begin. It is all timed up and Dr.
Jaims can walk out of the room while it
automatically plays.

Dr. Jaims walks back to the break room to
grab a cup of coffee and to talk with Dr. Blake and
Christie to come up with a game plan. As he walks
into the breakroom, he sees the extra slide deck
and slides spread across the breakroom table.
Christie hands him a cup of coffee and Dr. Jaims
says, "Good I can start loading the slide deck. My
plan is to start outside of the house and work our

way into the lower level and then upstairs. I want to lead his mind to the final slide of Jackie at the top of the stairs." Christie says, "I sure hope that sparks something with Aaron." Dr. Blake jumps into the conversation and says, "Remember the D.A. wants us to ask those specific questions." Christie looks surprised and says, "What questions?" Dr. Blake says, "Well, normally we would like Aaron to give the specifics and only ask open ended questions to get him to make descriptions that he remembers. But they want us to ask specifically about who pushed Jackie down the stairs and if the person is unknown to Aaron, they want to know about features that will solidify an arrest. Like tattoos, or scars that can still be incriminating features today." Christie says, "OK, that makes sense, I guess." Dr. Jaims says, "They also want us to ask if he remembers blood at all during the struggle." Christie says, "OK, that is weird because I don't remember any blood at the scene, but whatever helps." Dr. Jaims is busy loading up the slide deck and holds one up to the light. He says, "Dr. Blake, did you have this one tinted blue for some reason?" Dr. Blake says, "Yes, the blocks that Aaron played with also had a flash card in our memory set. The card showed BLOCKS as a blue card and Aaron told me once that when he played with blocks or Legos he would always envision blue highlights because of his synesthesia." Dr. Jaims said "Good, did you put a tint on any others just so I have a heads up?" Dr. Blake says, "Yes, the stairs are tinted sepia. We have one looking up the stairs, and the final slide with Jackie at the top of the stairs." Dr. Jaims says, "Great, that will help with the finale. I have them all set up in the slide deck. Let me go check on Aaron, the bedtime slides should be finishing."

Dr. Jaims walks into the control room to see how Aaron is doing and he sees the slides still flipping through toward the end and Aaron is asleep. So, Dr. Jaims hits pause on the CD and turns off the photo carousel. He carries the new slide deck into the session room and replaces the bedtime slides with the final session slide deck. He checks on Aaron before leaving him to sleep some. The vital sign probes are all in place and his pupil detection glasses are resting just right on his face with their green glow. All is well and they are set to let him sleep 2 hours before they start their final test after he hits REM sleep.

Chapter 27

Aaron's Final Test

Dr. Jaims, Christie, and Dr. Blake are all in the breakroom looking over the photo albums when Christie asks, "Will it be a while before we are testing Aaron?" Dr. Jaims looks at the clock on the wall and it reads 11:45pm. He says, "Well last night Aaron broke out of that first REM sleep when it was 12:30 am so we have some time before he is ready." Christie says, "I might try to grab some sleep before we start with Aaron. Will you guys wake me up when you start?" Dr. Blake says, "Yes, we will wake you up. There is a pull-out couch in session room B. It has already been pulled out and Mrs. Kawley put new linens on the bed today. It's all set up for you there." Christie says, "great I will get a little shut eye before we begin."

As Christie heads back to the room, Dr. Jaims figures he can get up and move around a bit now too. He is getting sleepy as well. He pours another cup of coffee and decides to check on the monitors in Dr. Blake's office. He walks in to see the 4 monitors are on live feed and Aaron is fast asleep. His heart rate and breathing indicate he is in REM sleep. The pupil detection glasses are actually showing his eyeball movement under his eyelids. This is a strong indication that REM sleep is in progress. It is possible that Aaron is in a dream state currently. Dr. Blake walks in the doorway and says, "There you are. I wondered where you went." Dr. Jaims said, "Take a look at his eye movement here on the green screen. He must be inside an intense dream right now. I wish we could see his thoughts on this monitor." Dr. Blake says, "That sure would be something, right?" Just then, they heard the front door buzzer sound and Dr. Blake pressed the intercom button, and said, "Hello, who is there?" The voice answers back, "It is Detective Jon Roberts, buzz me in." Dr. Blake hits the trigger to let him into the lobby.

Dr. Blake leaves the room to unlock his front office waiting room door and greets the Detective as he walks in. Dr. Blake says, "We are back in my office watching Aaron sleep right now." Detective Roberts says, "OK when do we begin?" Dr. Blake says, "We will begin here shortly." As they walk back, Dr. Blake offers him a cup of coffee and he accepts. He pours him a cup and says, "Let's go check on Aaron in my office on the LIVE feed monitors and get an update from Dr. Jaims." As they walk in to greet Dr. Jaims he stops them both in their tracks and says, "Aaron just started talking in his sleep. This is the best time to start his session. I know Christie just went back to bed but let her get some sleep, this may not even work to get him started. Let's see how it goes first."

Dr. Jaims walks into the session room quietly, flips on the projector, puts on his microphone, and grabs the projector remote control. He turns on the first slide that is loaded and puts his warm hand on Aaron. Just as his hand hits his shoulder Aaron says in a very sleepy voice, "Don't touch me." Dr. Jaims whispers, "OK Aaron, I will keep my hands to myself. Remember this is a safe place for you. And that all discussions are being recorded. Please acknowledge that we are OK to record this session today." Aaron says, "Yes that is OK!" He still hasn't opened his eyes. Dr. Jaims says, "Were you dreaming of something just now, Aaron?" Aaron doesn't answer so Dr. Jaims gives it a few seconds. Before he can begin, Aaron talks first. "Mom is that you?" Dr. Jaims is shocked at the question. Dr. Jaims decides to play along and says, "Yes Aaron, what are you doing?" Aaron says, "I'm playing with my blocks." Dr. Jaims quickly advances the slides to the playroom picture that shows Aaron's blocks as a kid. This picture was in the photo albums that Christie gave to Dr. Blake, and they tinted it Blue because of his synesthesia connected to a blue flash card. Dr. Jaims says, "Aaron, can you open your eyes and see your playroom on the ceiling? Are these your blocks?" Aaron slowly opens his eyes to see the scene on the ceiling." Aaron says, "Yes those are MY blue blocks, and they are not for you." Dr. Jaims says, "Don't worry Aaron, I won't touch your blocks. Can you tell me where your mom is right now." He says, "She is getting ready for her big date with daddy."

Dr. Jaims is stunned that it seems as if Aaron is already in the zone where he is back to the day Jackie was murdered. Aaron has said he dreams about that day sometimes and they must have gotten lucky that tonight was just one of those nights. Dr. Blake and Detective Roberts are in the office watching the monitors in amazement. Both men are speechless just watching in awe.

Dr. Jaims continues and asks, "Aaron, can we go back to the hallway now, outside of your bedroom." He takes the remote and flips to the slide of the stairway just outside of Jackie's room and the bathroom upstairs. Dr. Jaims says, "Are you in the hallway Aaron?" Aaron shakes his head yes in agreement. Before Dr. Jaims can continue Aaron says, "Mommy I'm scared." Dr. Jaims says, "Its ok honey, just follow me. What do you see now down the hallway to the stairs?" Aaron starts to wince and says, "Uncle Greg is here to give me a hug." Dr. Jaims says, "Are you still scared Aaron?" Aaron says, "No it was just Uncle Greg, and he tells me to go back to playing so I'm going back now." Dr. Jaims says, "Can you stay in the hallway, Aaron?" Aaron replies, "No I have to play with my blocks."

Dr. Blake is looking at the monitor with Detective Roberts and Dr. Blake says, "He has to keep him out near Jackie." Detective Roberts says, "Well maybe he never left his toy room that night." Dr. Blake says, "I have studied his journal entries for years. I believe he was there to see it all. I just have a feeling." They can hear Dr. Jaims continue in the session room and turn up the volume on the monitors. Dr. Jaims says, "Aaron, can you go back to the hallway for me?" Dr. Jaims flips a few slides to the photo of Jackie on the stairs in a sepia tinted slide. Sepia is Aaron's synesthesia connection to stairs. Aaron says, "Mommy is hurt." Dr. Jaims eyes get big and he says, "Why is mommy hurt Aaron?" He says, "Mommy and Greg are hurting." Dr. Jaims says, "Do you hear something to make you think they are hurting, Aaron?" Aaron says, "Yes Mommy is moaning like maybe she is hurt, and Uncle Greg is on top of her in the bed under the covers. She keeps asking him to do it harder and please Greg dont stop, right there. They are really moving the blankets around. Maybe Mommy fell off the bed? Dr. Jaims says, "What do you see now, Aaron?" Aaron says, "Greg sees me and yells at me to go play in my room." Dr. Jaims says, "Ok Aaron, go back to your blocks in the playroom." Aaron says, "OK but I hear them fighting now." Dr. Jaims says, "Can you hear what they are saying Aaron?" Aaron says, "Yes, mommy told Greg not to yell at me, that I am just a child. She is telling Greg that he cannot be with her anymore. She is in love with Melvin. Melvin is my dad." Dr. Jaims says, "Yes Aaron, Melvin is your father. Is your father there." Aaron says, "No dad is not here right now, he is at work." Dr. Jaims still has the slide of Jacklyn on the stairs in sepia on the ceiling. He asks Aaron, "Please open your eyes Aaron and look at the image on the ceiling for me." Aaron slowly opens his eyes. Dr. Blake sees that his pupils are at 95% dilated on the monitor. He is taking in all the image with his eyes now. He closes his eyes again and Dr. Jaims says, "Aaron can you see Greg pushing your mommy?" Aaron says, "No I am in the playroom, but I am listening." He opens his eyes and Dr. Jaims asks, "Can you see mommy now?" Dr. Blake is fixed on the pupil monitor, and the dilation percentage is at 35% so Dr. Blake believes from past sessions that he is using his Eidetic recall more than what is shown in the image to tell the story now. Aaron answers, "I am in the playroom with my blocks, but I am listening. They have moved to the bathroom, and I can't hear them as well. I am moving to the hallway to hear better." Dr. Jaims says, "What do you see now Aaron?" Aaron says, "There is a strange man in the hallway now." Dr. Jaims says, "Is the strange man Greg?" Aaron says, "No this man has black clothes on with a mask over his face. He says to me, "Get going kid, go to your playroom." Then he got into the closet." Dr. Jaims says, "Who is this Man Aaron?" Aaron says, "I don't know this man. He scares me." Dr. Jaims says, "Can you see any scars on this man or tattoos?" This is when Detective Roberts looks to Dr. Blake and says, "There it is, Bryce will be happy when he hears that question on playback tomorrow." Aaron says, "No his skin is all covered, but I can see that he has long black hair sticking out of the back of his mask when he turns to get into the closet." Dr. Jaims says, "What do you do now?" Aaron says, "I am scared of that man in the closet, so I run to my playroom." Dr. Jaims says, "Aaron can you still hear Greg and mommy fighting?" Aaron says, "Yes, they are back in the hallway. But the fighting stopped." Dr. Jaims fears the worst and says, "Why did the fighting stop Aaron?" Aaron says, "The phone in the hallway rang and mommy picked it up." She is closer to the playroom now and I can hear her talking to Daddy. She tells him to hurry home." Dr. Jaims asks, "Is she off the phone yet Aaron?" Aaron said, "I don't know it is quiet again. Should I look for mommy?" Dr. Jaims says, "Yes Aaron see if you can find Mommy." Just then Aaron begins to cry, "Mommy is fighting with the man again." Dr. Jaims says, "What man Aaron, can you tell me more?" Aaron looks to be in deep thought and then he replies, "I can't tell. It's a man dressed in black again?" Dr. Jaims asks, "Is it the man wearing the mask again?" Aaron says, "I can't tell what he is wearing, it is dark, but he just said OUCH shit that hurt with his hands over his mouth." Dr. Jaims says, "The man got hurt?" Aaron says, "Yes he bumped his nose, and I see a lot of blood on the wall by the stairs." Dr. Jaims says, "You see blood? Good Aaron, can you see what stairs have the blood?" Aaron says, "It's all over the wall and baseboard at the top of the steps, but the man is cleaning it up right now." Dr. Jaims says, "Aaron, do you see mommy anywhere?" Aaron says, "No mommy is gone. The man is running to the bathroom with rags to clean up the blood. He screams loudly and I am scared. I am going back to the toy room until mom comes back. I am really scared." Dr. Jaims says, "Aaron before you go can you see the man again." Aaron says, "No, his screaming is scaring me, I want to hide in the toy room."

Dr. Blake decides to press the microphone button in the session room, and he says "Brian, I think we have enough, let Aaron get some rest." Dr. Jaims agrees and he tells Aaron, "Stay calm Aaron, you did great work, fall fast asleep and we will continue after the short break." Aaron already had his eyes closed but you can see that he is calming down and falling fast asleep. Dr. Jaims stands up and walks out with his hands and feet numb after that session of back and forth with Aaron.

He gets back to the monitor room and Detective Roberts applauds his efforts and says, "Wow Doc, that was incredible once again tonight! You really hit it out of the park with Aaron on that one." Dr. Jaims says, "I really cannot believe that he happened to be dreaming of the murder tonight. Finding him talking in his sleep before I even went in there, just presented the perfect opportunity for us to take advantage of the situation." Dr. Blake says, "Christie is going to be pissed that we didn't wake her up but now that I heard what Aaron witnessed that night, I am glad she wasn't here."

Just then Christie walked into the room. Rubbing the sleep out of her eyes she said, "Did you guys start without me?" They all looked stunned, and Dr. Blake said, "UH, no we were just testing the lighting in the room and getting the microphone setup on Dr. Jaims." Dr. Jaims says, "Uh yeah, Aaron has been tossing and turning so

we have been putting off waking him up just yet."
Detective Roberts says, "Hi Christie, I just got here
so I am, ah, ready for action. And to be honest, I
must hit the restroom before we begin." He walks
out of the room and Christie walks over to view the
monitors. She looks hard at Aaron and can see that
his cheeks are wet in the green glow from his pupil
dilation glasses. She asks, "Has Aaron been crying,
his cheeks look to be wet." Dr. Jaims says, "I don't
think so, he was mumbling in his sleep just a few
moments ago. He could be dreaming." She says,
"Well his cheeks look wet, I just hope he is OK." Dr.
Jaims says, "I was just in there checking on him and
he seems fine. His temperature is normal, and his
vital signs are perfect. Christie says, "Is it OK if I go
in and watch him sleep for a little bit?" Dr. Blake
says, "Yes that is totally fine. Dr. Jaims and I have
to go back to the breakroom and plan out this first
session with Aaron, so we don't forget anything.
Christie goes in and sits in the chair next to Aaron.
She is quietly listening to his breathing.

Dr. Jaims and Dr. Blake go out to the
breakroom. Dr. Blake says, "Boy that was a close
one!" Dr. Jaims says, "You're telling me." Dr. Blake
continues, "Hey, I'm gonna go give Bryce Edwards a
quick update. Can you hold down the fort for a few
minutes?" Dr. Jaims says, "Sure, tell him I said Hi. I
will just be here making a fresh pot of coffee."

Dr. Blake leaves and then Christie walks into
the breakroom. She says, "You know what Dr.
Jaims?" He says, "What is it Christie?" She says, "I

am sure you have heard it before, but you are a good-looking man! If it weren't for Greg, you'd be in trouble mister." Dr. Jaims just laughs and says, "You are right, I have heard it all before." She laughs and says, "Well, while I sat there watching Aaron sleep, I have decided that I don't want to be here to witness him relive the day Jackie died. I called Greg and asked him to pick me up." Dr. Jaims says, "Really, that is too bad because you will miss out on the magic show I am about to create with Aaron." Christie says, "Yeah, like I said I really don't want to see that, it will be too much for me tonight."

Just then they heard the buzzer ring in the front lobby and Greg was already here. Dr. Jaims says, "Well at least let me walk you out." They walk to Dr. Blake's office and answer the buzzer over the intercom. Christie pushes the button and says, "Hello." Greg answers, "Babe, it's me and it's cold out here. Get your chicken legs down here asap." Dr. Jaims says, "Right this way young lady." He walks her down to the lobby, unlocks the door and lets her head out with Greg. He locks up and walks back to Dr. Blake's office in silence thinking about what they had just discovered about Greg and Jackie.

Chapter 28

Late Night Phone Calls

      Detective Roberts walks to a squad car parked just outside Dr. Blake's office where he gets in and shuts the door. He reaches into his front pants pocket and pulls out a cellphone. He flips it open and tries to dial the former DA, Ben Henke. His hands are shaking a little bit from Aaron's story, and he can't press the correct numbers. He can't believe that he would remember about the blood. He finally dials the number, and Ben answers. Detective Roberts says, "Ben, we've got problems. The kid remembers some blood from his mom's killer when she got pushed down the stairs." Ben looks at the time on his side table clock next to his bed. It reads 1:15am and he says, "Alright. Well, where did he say he saw this, Blood?" Detective Roberts says, "He said, he busted his nose at the top of the stairs, and the blood dripped behind a baseboard, possibly. He said the killer cleaned it up, so nobody could see it but there are probably still remnants of blood behind that baseboard." Ben sits up on the side of his bed and says, "I doubt that would incriminate someone this many years later, but we need you to go and check it out before the DA does. There is no way they will be getting a search warrant this late tonight so let's make a plan to meet with George at the 88th Street Diner, so we can discuss the plan to cover this up. How does 9AM sound?" Detective Roberts says, "That's fine. I'll meet you guys there. In the meantime, I'll get some more details on what they're going to do about this. And we can make our own plans around that."

At around the same time that Detective Roberts was out making his phone call, Dr. Blake puts in a call to the new DA, Bryce Edwards. Dr. Blake dials the phone and Bryce picks up. Dr. Blake says, "Bryce, is that you?" Bryce says, "Yes. I'm here, Dr. Blake. What's the good news?" Doctor Blake says, "Well, we had a good night with Aaron. He's telling us there's some blood possibly behind a baseboard at the top of the stairs where his Mom had fallen. We think if you remove the baseboard there could be some blood evidence." Bryce tells him, "Well, I'm not going to waste any time. I'm going there with forensics now, and we're going to get a sample to the lab ASAP." Dr. Blake told him, "Good luck! And we'll keep going with Aaron to see what else we can find out. So far, this seems like a good start?" Bryce says, "You better believe it! I'll call you when I find some blood."

Dr. Blake hangs up the phone and feels good about what they've done with Aaron. He walks back to join Dr. Jaims in the lunchroom. He asks, Dr. Jaims, "What are we going to do next with Aaron?" Dr. Jaims says, "Well for now we're going to let him rest a little bit. That was rough on the kid. We'll give him about 2 hours of rest and maybe we'll see if he can get past his REM sleep. We need some more credibility with this technique. So, we need to ask him about when he went to see his grandmother in the hospital. If we can get some information from him from that day, and it proves to be true, then we have at least four events that we can pull from to show that this technique is working with Aaron. Usually this helps convince a jury." Dr. Blake says, "Is anybody hungry? I know a good Chinese place that delivers late. I'll put an order." Dr. Jaims says, "No, I think I'm good." Just then Dr. Blake realized that neither Detective Roberts nor Christie was in the room. He asks Dr. Jaims, "Do you know where Det. Roberts is hiding?" And Dr. Jaims says, "I have no idea. Last I saw he was watching the monitors." Dr. Blake says, "Well, maybe he just stepped outside for a cigarette or something, or to make a phone call." Dr. Jaims says, "And Christie called Greg to come pick her up." Dr. Blake says, "Is everything alright?" Dr. Jaims says, "All is good, she just didn't want to be present to hear about her sister being killed through the mind of her nephew." Dr. Blake looked over at Dr. Jaims and said, "Well she already missed that party."

Chapter 29

Kathy Dunbar's Collection

Bryce takes the last drink of his 30-year-old aged Whiskey. He decides to pick up the phone in his living room and he gives a call to the forensics office down at the county municipal building. When the call goes through, he asks for Kathy Dunbar, Chief Coroner. He's patched through to Kathy, and when she answers she says, without saying hello, "This better be good because I'm off in about 10 minutes." Bryce says, "Well hello, Kat." Everyone calls her Kat, because she is a multiple cat owner and is proud of it. Bryce continues, "It's Bryce calling again. I know we've talked about eight times today, but this is a good one. Who you got working the late shift that can meet me at 1415 Penny Stream Lane?" Kat says, "Nobody at this hour. Why, what's going on?" Bryce says, "Well, we have to go pick up some blood evidence in a murder case." Kat replies, "Is this a murder case that happened recently or is this one from a legacy file? Bryce says, "It's on an old, solved case…. Jacklyn Casey." Kat says, "I thought we solved that 10 years ago. It was her husband, Melvin Casey." Bryce says, "Well, we got an anonymous tip that there's some blood at the scene." Kat laughs and says, "Blood from 10 years ago? I'm not sure that's gonna fly." Bryce says, "Just humor me and have somebody meet me at the address." Kat says, "Well, I've got nobody so I'll meet you there." Bryce says, "Okay. I'll be there in 15 minutes."

Bryce hangs up the phone, runs out the door with his briefcase, and he hits the freeway as quick as he can.

Once Bryce gets to the house, he sees that Kat's already there, and she is driving the meat wagon. It is an early 90's Ford Econoline with "King County Coroner" written down both sides. They both get out of their vehicles at the same time. Kat looks over Bryce and says, "This better be good! I have a cat that's waiting for me to get home." Bryce looks at her and says, "You only have one cat now? That's hard for me to believe!" She looks at him and says, "Shut up. You're right. I've got three waiting on me to get home. Let's just get this over with."

Bryce and Kat walk up the steps onto the porch and ring the doorbell. Greg and Christie answer the door together. Bryce speaks first, "Hi there folks, we are here on behalf of the Seattle Police Department. I am the District Attorney Bryce Edwards, and this is Kathy Dunbar, Chief Coroner and the Director of Forensics. We understand that you are the legal guardians of Aaron Casey?" This is when Christie jumps in and says, "Yes, we are, and Aaron is not here right now." Bryce says, "Yes, we know. Aaron is the reason we are here. He has passed along information to the team that we can recover some evidence at the top of your staircase. With your permission we would like to collect a sample from the location he has revealed to us." Now Greg jumps in on the conversation, "Don't you need a search warrant for this type of situation?" Bryce says, "Normally yes, but with this evidence it could free Melvin Casey and relieve Aaron of more nights away from home. We were hoping you would sign this affidavit that allows us to collect the evidence with your permission as the homeowners. This would negate the need to secure a search warrant." Christie says, "Greg, sign the damn paper and let them do their jobs!" Greg signs the paper, and Christie grabs the clipboard and signs the paper as well.

Bryce says, "Thank you, we will be out of your hair here within the next 30 minutes. Just show us to the staircase and we will be looking to take some of the base board as evidence." Greg says, "You need to take the baseboard with you?" Kat jumps in and says, "Yes Mr. Flint. I apologize, we will need to remove a portion of the baseboard, and we will not be able to return it." Greg looks back at Christie and says, "Babe, they want to take the baseboard with them. Are you OK with that? I will have to go to Home Depot this weekend and replace it. You know that paint won't be easy to match. We're gonna have to paint the whole damn stairway baseboard and that color runs the full hallway upstairs too." Christie says, "Oh calm down, it all needs new paint anyways. Last time we painted Aaron was still in diapers!" They get to the area where Aaron indicated and determine they will have to take the strip from the closest doorway to halfway down the stairs. Bryce takes the Sawzall and goes to cut halfway down the stairs and Greg decides to stop him. Greg says, "Mister D.A., ah I mean Bryce. Why don't you just remove all the baseboard going down the stairs. That seam is gonna annoy the shit out of me every day going down the steps. I will just replace the full length with one piece." Bryce agrees, and before they start Kat asks to take a photo of it installed before it is removed. After the photos they removed the full length of the stairs and the 4-foot section at the top that ran from the staircase to the first doorway. Once removed Kat took her camera and snapped some photos of the baseboard's backside. It is clear to everyone that the board extending to the doorway has blood stains and the piece going down the stairs has stains at the top two steps. She marks the blood stains with evidence indicators and takes 4 photos. Kat says, "It looks like Aaron was right with his memory of blood getting behind these baseboards. We will take these with us and move to getting them DNA tested asap." Greg asks to help get the pieces out to the van and Kat quickly lets him know they will have to wrap the pieces in plastic and that only Bryce and her can collect the evidence. Then Kat looks at the wall and realizes they will need to cut out part of the drywall as evidence as well. She points at the stains on the wall and looks at Greg. She says, "Greg, unfortunately we will have to collect that drywall as well." Greg says, "Oh you have got to be kidding me. It looks like my weekend is booked up now Babe. Drywall and baseboards, my two favorites."

Kat and Bryce get it all collected, labeled, and in the van for transport to the Forensics lab. They close the van up and Kat looks at Bryce and says, "How did we miss this the first time?" Bryce says, "I am not sure it would have even mattered. Let's just get it right this time." Kat says, "Is there something you are not telling me here Bryce?" He says, "This is not the time, but I will let you know the situation in the morning." Kat says, "Alright, I am out. See you tomorrow, I've got it from here."

Chapter 30

Bryce Edwards Calls Det. Roberts

It's 6am the morning after the blood discovery, the new DA Bryce Edwards shuts off his alarm clock and is excited to find out the results on this DNA recovered from the Flint household. He decides to call Kathy Dunbar as soon as he sits up out of bed to find out if she has results yet. He grabs his phone off his bedside table and sees he already has 3 texts from her. He opens his phone and reveals that she has written, "Good Morning Bryce, the DNA evidence has proven to NOT match Melvin Casey's. We ran it through the FBI's CODIS program, and it is not matching anyone in the system at this time. We will need fresh suspects on this one to find a match." Bryce closes his phone and says to himself out loud, "Damn it! Well at least we can possibly help Melvin with this discovery."

Just then his phone began to ring. He sees it is Detective Jon Roberts. He answers, "Bryce Edwards here." The detective begins, "Hey Bryce. How are you this morning?" Bryce answers, "Doing well, we just found out blood from the scene does not match Melvin Casey!" Detective Roberts is stunned and says, "Wait, you already collected the blood at the Flint residence? When did this happen?" Bryce says, "Kat and I went and collected it last night, there is no time to spare in this kind of investigation." The detective jumps back in and says, "How did you get a search warrant that late at night?" Bryce says, "Well we figured Aaron's family wants to free Melvin, so we just asked for permission, and they allowed our search and collection on the scene. They signed a waiver, and we got in and out of there in less than an hour." Detective Roberts seems upset when he says, "Bryce, this is my case to break open! I can't believe you would do this behind my back!" In a worrisome tone Detective Roberts continues, "If the DNA does not match Melvin Casey, then who did it match?" Bryce Edwards can feel the detective has some nerves behind this question for some reason. He decides to not tell the whole truth here and says, "Well, Kat ran the DNA in the FBI CODIS database and the system is still searching at this time. If we get a hit I will call and let you know." Detective Roberts is back to being angry with Bryce and says, "I still cannot believe you did this without telling me Bryce. I know this DA role is new to you, but you have to keep me in the loop with investigations, especially when I am running as the lead detective. Don't go rogue on me anymore, you hear me?!" Bryce agrees and says, "OK OK. Calm down, I didn't think it was that big of a deal. I will keep you in the loop from now on." Detective Roberts says, "OK, well if anything hits on that CODIS search let me know and I will see you on Monday!" Bryce agrees and hangs up the call, but he is wondering why he was so upset that he wasn't there to help collect the blood evidence.

Bryce decides to call Chief Pavlock for help. Bryce dials his phone and hears it ringing. "Chief Pavlock here and this better be good on a Sunday to interrupt my golf game." Bryce speaks up, "Hey Chief, I need a quick favor." The Chief answers quickly, "You just started as DA and you're already needing a favor from me? This is gonna be a long 4-year term Bryce. What do you need from me while I am in the middle of the golf course?" Bryce says, "I need you to follow Detective Jon Roberts for the next couple days. I need to track his movements. He's acting weird on the Melvin Casey investigation. I think he was involved somehow." The Chief answers, "Jon is a standup guy. I will get a tail on him, but I am telling you it won't bear any fruit." Bryce says, "I hope you are right on this one. I will let you go, hit 'em straight Chief." Bryce hangs up the phone and decides to start his usual Sunday with a 3-mile run and some bacon and eggs.

Chapter 31

Bryce Calls Dr. Blake

Bryce is just coming home from his 3-mile run around his neighborhood. He takes off his running shoes and begins to prepare his kitchen for cooking breakfast. Bryce is a single man that has been dedicated to serving the public as a defense attorney for the last 12 years. His first year as a lawyer landed him a job at the Casey Worthington Mitchell law office where partner Nolan Mitchell was his mentor. He knew Melvin Casey for only a few years before he was convicted of killing Jacklyn. Breaking this case open has a bittersweet feeling for him. He wants to free Melvin, but he also doesn't know what it will boil up in this decade long pot of corruption.

Bryce decides to give Dr. Blake a call to give him an update and to warn him about Detective Roberts. The phone rings and Dr. Blake sees that it is Bryce Edwards on the face of his cellphone, so he answers, "Hello Bryce, I hope you slept well." Bryce answers, "Oh, you know it. Just like a baby. Listen Dr. Blake, we received the results back from the DNA collection and we have found out it does NOT match Melvin Casey!" Dr. Blake says, "That is GREAT news! Have you told Aaron or his family yet?" Bryce says, "No not yet! We are holding the findings to investigate further into who it could have been. Please do not share this information with them just yet. We are very concerned that Aaron has revealed his Uncle Greg Flint was having an affair with his mother, Jacklyn Casey. This information proves that Greg has motive in the case and he is now a suspect." Dr. Blake says, "Ah, that makes sense, I will not say anything to anyone just yet." Bryce continues, "I wanted to call and warn you about Detective Roberts. He became very upset with me when I told him we had collected the blood evidence already and it does not match with Melvin Casey. I am unsure if he was involved with this case, but I am having him followed just to clear him of any suspicious activity for the short term. Be very careful about what you say around him until I can clear him from the investigation. If he contacts, you today please let me know as soon as possible." Dr. Blake says, "Thank you for the heads up and I will reach out if I hear from him at all."

Chapter 32

The 88th St. Diner Boys

Well, it is 8:45 and Detective Jon Roberts is waiting in the usual booth at the 88th St. Diner. It's Sunday morning and the diner is fairly busy. While this is not good for having this kind of conversation, Detective Roberts hopes it will keep the conversation somewhat civilized.

Detective Roberts takes a sip of his coffee and out of the corner of his eye he sees Ben Henke walking in with his hitman/muscle, George Gallapolos. Ben takes a seat across from Detective Roberts and George tells the Detective to scoot over and he sits next to him. This puts Detective Roberts on edge. He has never liked George, one because his long black hair is always so greasy and two because of the knowledge he has about what he would do to those that get in his way. George puts his arm around the Detective and says, "Hey Jon, how've you been? I've missed yah!" Jon says, "Come on get your hands off me. I am not in uniform, but someone might recognize me." Ben says, "Cut it out you two! We need a plan, what did you find out so far Jon?" Detective Roberts says, "Well they already collected the blood evidence and it's not Melvin's." George looks at Ben and says, "I thought he was supposed to be there when they collected the blood evidence to cover it up!" Ben looks over at Detective Roberts and says, "Yeah, how did they collect this evidence without you being there to cover it up! Are you trying to get us caught!" Before Detective Roberts can even answer Ben takes off his sunglasses and looks straight into George's eyes. Before he says anything, Detective Roberts sees that he has a nasty black eye. Ben says, "Tell me straight to my face. Is the blood yours? We need to know now before it blows up in our face George!" George says, "NO, it ain't my blood. Guys like me don't leave evidence at the scene of a crime! I'm a professional!"

Detective Roberts swallows hard now realizing these two put the muscle to a couple junior high kids in the woods. Detective Roberts shakes it off and says, "They told me they entered the DNA evidence into the FBI CODIS database and the search was still running at the time. I don't know if they have a hit yet or not." Ben Henke says, "Shit, George's DNA is in the system from his first conviction. Its gonna hit, if it's his." George speaks up, "I'm telling you man, it ain't my blood! It takes a lot to make me bleed and that boney bitch didn't see me coming when I pushed her down the stairs!" Ben says, "Well its somebody's blood and we have to cover our bases so Jon you better keep your nose to the grindstone!" Ben looks to George and says, "Let's go figure out Plan C where it's not so crowded, and Jon you better report back by Noon today!"

As George and Ben walk out of the diner the undercover cop that is following Detective Roberts for Chief Pavlock is snapping photographs of the two leaving the diner. He waits while they have a conversation outside of their car. While they are talking Detective Jon Roberts walks up to them and hands them something. While they are all together the undercover cop gets multiple shots of the three of them talking. This is key evidence the undercover cop is now uploading to his phone and then to the cloud linked to the Chief. The chief gets a notification on his phone of the upload. Before he takes his putt on the 14th hole, he opens the image to reveal the detective talking with Ben Henke and George Gallapolos. He shakes his head in disgust and says, "Fuck!" The other guys in his foursome say, "Chief, you alright?" He says, "Yeah, just got some bad news about a good guy! Now look out and let me knock down this putt."

Chapter 33

Bryce Visits Melvin Casey

Melvin Casey was being walked down to the visitor's cell by a Prison guard. When he arrives at the visitor's cell he is surprised to see an old friend. He looks in as they open the cell door and says, "Bryce is that you?" Bryce stands up and says, "Yes, it is Melvin, how are you?" Mel answers, "Well I've been better. What are you here for?" Bryce says, "Sit down Mel, I have some good news and some bad news. Using photo elicitation therapy, Aaron has remembered the day Jackie died and he saw two men and neither of them were you! We also recovered some DNA evidence that he located with his Eidetic Rehab Sessions with Dr. Jaims. That kid's memory is spot on!" Mel jumps in and says, "This all sounds like good news to me, what is the bad news?" Bryce says, "Well it is not enough to instantly get you out of jail. We need more evidence to create a re-trial. So far, the DNA evidence has been proven to not match you; however, it doesn't create a hit on the FBI's CODIS database. We need a suspect to test positive for it to be solid evidence in the case."

Melvin decides to steer Bryce into a new direction and says, "Well Bryce, I have been holding the following information from investigators because they were threatening to kill Aaron if I ever told. I have a deposit box down at Metro Bank on 6th Street. It's the bank across the street from my old law firm. I put Christie down as a joint owner of the box just in case something happened. Inside the box is all the evidence you will need to put all the players away for a long time, including Ben Henke. It shows 6 instances of trial manipulation with falsified plea deals making for 6 successful convictions. This made the District Attorney a huge success over that span of time, and usually it hit right when he needed to be re-elected. My case would be the 7th with the false testimony of Angie VanPatton. I am sure they forced her to lie in my trial threatening harm to her or her daughter down in Portland." So, take Christie down to the bank and break into that box for the remainder of the evidence you need. Just keep Aaron, Christie, and Greg in a safe house until all the players are in custody." Bryce looks Melvin in the eyes and says, "Mel, I will owe you on this one my friend." Mel, with a big grin on his face, says, "Just get me out of this cage and I will call it even."

Chapter 34

Bryce at the Flint Household

Bryce leaves the prison and decides to call Kat at the coroner's office before he gets to the Flint Household. He tells the receptionist that he needs Kathy Dunbar, the Chief Coroner. She patches him through and Kat answers, "Hello this is Kathy Dunbar." Bryce says, "Hello Kat, It's Bryce Edwards. I need another favor from you." Kat says, "What is it now? Did you find some blood evidence that will get John Wilkes Booth off for shooting President Lincoln?" Bryce has to laugh at that one and says, "Whatever Kat! Just let me know if you can meet me back at the Flint Residence within half hour?" Kat says, "Why, what is happening now?" Bryce says, "Greg Flint needs to be eliminated as a suspect just to keep the investigation clean. We need him to furnish some DNA to clear him of involvement because Aaron has placed him at the crime scene during his Eidetic Rehab assignment with Dr. Jaims." Kat says, "OK I will be right over with a DNA collection kit. Are you sure he will furnish his DNA without a warrant? I don't really want to waste my time driving over if he gives a denial." Bryce says, "If he's got nothing to hide, he will consent." Kat agrees, grabs the kit and hits the road.

Bryce pulls into Flint's driveway. He walks up to the house and sees that Christie and Greg are sitting on the front porch with glasses of tea in their hands. Christie says, "Bryce Edwards, is that you? We are up here on the porch drinking sweet tea. Do you want me to pour you a glass for your visit." He says, "Sure that sounds great right now." Greg speaks up from his rocking chair as the DA walks up the stairs to the porch. He says, "We like to enjoy days like this when it doesn't rain here in Seattle. You can't let 'em go to waste!" Bryce says, "That's a fact." Greg says, "What brings you to our side of town? You already took our baseboard, are you looking for some railing this time?" Bryce said, "Oh no, just here to talk with you and Christie. I will wait for her to come back before I begin." Just then Christie comes out carrying that glass of tea for Bryce. He says, "Thank you so much Christie." He takes a sip and says, "Oh boy, that is good. Hey, let me get to why I am here. I went to the prison and talked to Melvin today. He gave me some good news. He has a deposit box at Metro Bank containing some evidence that I will use to help close the case and it could possibly get him out of prison." Christie said, "Oh wow, that is great. What can we do to help?" Bryce says, "Well he put the deposit box in his name with Christie as a joint owner. I will need you to be there when I collect the contents of the box. I have called the bank, and they said they will have a private room reserved for our use to clean out the box in 30 minutes from now. If you are free, I would like you to ride over there with me."

Just then from the porch they see Kathy Dunbar pull up to the house in the Coroner Van. She climbs out of the van carrying a DNA collection kit. Bryce says, "Oh yeah and Greg I need Kat here to collect some of your DNA to eliminate you as a suspect." Greg sits up quickly and says, "What the hell, why am I a suspect?" Bryce says, "Well Aaron's eidetic rehab assignment placed you at the scene when Jackie was killed." Greg said, "Yes I was there, but I was there to pick up Aaron for the weekend and that is when I found Jackie dead at the bottom of the stairs!" Bryce says, "We know Greg, but it will still be required just to eliminate you without a shadow of a doubt since that DNA evidence in the stairway is still not linked to anyone at the crime scene." Greg says, "Whatever, that is fine she can stick me right here on the porch, I'm not moving from this spot. You guys go do your bank thing." Bryce and Christie start down the stairs and pass Kat on their way down. Bryce tells her, "He gave us consent to the DNA collection. We are running to the bank. We will be right back." Kat says, "I don't take 50s or 100s so make sure my tip is in smaller bills." Christie laughs and says, "HA, Good luck with Greg, he hates needles."

Bryce and Christie get to the bank and the head teller escorts them to the private room where the box was already removed from the vault and was waiting for them to be opened. The teller says, "You have until 12:50 to collect what you need, and we will put the box back when you are finished. I assume you have the access code to the box?" Bryce says, "Yes we have the code." The teller says, "OK, lock it up when you are finished, and we will take care of putting the box back in the vault. Please remember that this door to the room can be opened from the inside but will be locked from the outside. So, when you exit you will not be allowed to re-enter. Make sure when you leave you have everything you need. I will now give you some privacy, have a good day if I don't see you before you leave." Bryce says, "Thank you" as she closes the door. Bryce looks at the clock on the wall and they have 25 minutes to clean the box. He enters the code on the digital pin pad on the box. He hears the lock click open and he lifts the lid to see neatly stacked files. He shuffles through them quickly and sees the 6 cases that Melvin mentioned. He takes them all out of the box and sits them on the table. He begins to look at the first file just to get an idea of what he has. That is when he sees Christie looking in the box. She says, "What is this note in the bottom of the box?" She opens the folded note and reads it out loud. In Melvin's handwriting it says, "Dear Christie, if you are reading this note that probably means I am dead. I want you to know that I forgive Greg for having an affair with Jacklyn, and you should too." Christie looks over at Bryce and says, "What in the hell is this about?" Bryce says, "You were asleep when Aaron revealed in his hypnotic state that Greg was at the house not only to pick him up for the weekend, but he was there being intimate with her before she was killed." At that moment, Bryce's cell phone started to ring. He says to Christie, "This is Kat, I have to take this." He answers and says, "Hey Kat, what is up." Kat says, "He gave a denial, like I told you he would. First, he said he didn't like needles and then when I told him I could take a hair sample or mouth swab he straight up refused. We are going to need a warrant." Bryce said, "OK I will work on it when I leave here." He hangs up and Christie says, "That bastard didn't give his DNA, did he?" Bryce said, "No he didn't." Christie says, "He didn't kill my sister, did he?" Bryce says, "We don't know yet Christie until we can eliminate him with his DNA." She is about to blow up when she says, "Get what you need and let's go. I'm gonna kill him when we get back!" Bryce has one more thing to tell her before they leave. Bryce locks up the box and puts the files in the bag the bank provided and says to her, "Christie we need to get you, Greg, and Aaron to a safe house for a couple days. Melvin says when we announce the contents of these files you will not be safe until we apprehend everyone involved." She said, "Greg may need his own safe house when I get home, we are fucking through! I am going to divorce his ass! I can't believe he was sleeping with my sister! Melvin won't get off easy either, he knew this whole time and didn't tell me!" Bryce says, "Ok let's go and get you guys packed for a mini vacation."

They arrive back at the Flint household and see the garage is open. Christie runs up into the house and yells, "Aaron, are you upstairs!" Aaron yells back down, "Yes, I am up in my room!" Christie says, "Get down here so I can talk to you!" He runs downstairs and says, "What is going on?" Christie says, "Where is Greg, his bike is gone!" Aaron says, "I don't know. He was acting weird and gave me a hug and said he was going on a bike ride." Christie looks over to Bryce and says, "If you can collect any DNA evidence in the house you are free to make a collection here. Hairs in the bed, or from a brush of his. His toothbrush or one of the 4 motorcycle helmets he has in the garage. Collect some things and have Kat test them. That bastard can run but he can't hide!" Bryce says, "I will collect a few of those items and take them to Kat at the coroner's office. Once we get a warrant, I will have Kat run some DNA tests. We will get to the bottom of this. For now, I need you and Aaron to pack up 3 days' worth of clothes and come with me to a safe house until this mess blows over. Aaron says, "I'm not going to sleep in my own bed again tonight?" Bryce says, "Nope, but I have a surprise for you. Miley and her family need to stay in the same safe house during this time so you will not be alone in this mini vacation." Aaron gets excited and says, "OK let me grab my stuff quickly, I'll meet you at the car." Bryce said, "I'm going down to inform the Sanders they need to come with us to the safe house for a few days."

While Bryce is walking down to the Sanders' residence, he calls in another squad car to pick up the Sanders family. The Sanders family was scared when they heard the news, but they agreed that the safe house is the best option at this time until the arrests are made. Bryce heads back to his squad car and starts the engine. He sits and waits in the driveway for Christie and Aaron to get ready. They both eventually come up and throw their bags in the trunk of the car and head to the safe house. The Sanders family is right behind them.

Chapter 35

The Safe House

Aaron was unpacking his bag in his bedroom at the safe house when Miley stopped by to say Hi. She stepped into his doorway and said, "Hey you, how are you doing?" Aaron said, "OK I guess." Miley said, "Kinda strange that they are putting us up in this house while they arrest all the bad guys. What did you tell them in your therapy, it must have been something good to open this can of worms!" Aaron raised his eyebrows and said, "Yeah I guess." Miley said, "What's going on Aaron, why do you seem so sad." Aaron says, "Well the last two nights of therapy has me remembering more than I ever imagined." Miley said, "Really, like what?" Aaron says, "Well my Nana for example. I remember when she was dying in the hospital. She told me that she was going away for a while and that I had to take care of my mom for her. I failed her Miley. I couldn't save my mom from that killer. I was there and all I could do was hide when it was her darkest hour. Miley said, "You were 2 years old against a grown man! What were you supposed to do, Aaron?" Aaron says, "I don't know I could have done something more than just hide in the corner."

Miley says, "Well you are doing something now Aaron and that counts for something!" Aaron says, "Yeah, I guess so. But now they say it could be Uncle Greg because of what I said during my session."

Christie is unpacking her bag when Bryce peeks in and says, "Hey Christie can I borrow you for a minute, we need to talk." Christie says, "Sure, Bryce. But I'm still mad at you for not telling me about Greg's affair." Bryce says, "I will make it up to you somehow, just meet me in the kitchen when you have a second." Bryce walks away and Christie finishes up putting away some of her clothes in the dressers. She can't help but wonder if he is asking to talk to her because the DNA collection from Greg has been tested against the blood at the scene. She gets to a point where she can walk away and works her way down to the kitchen. She hears a female voice as she gets closer to the kitchen and it's not Mrs. Sanders. She walks into the room and it's Bryce talking to Angie VanPatton and her daughter. Christie interrupts, "What the hell are they doing here?" Angie looks over to Christie as she is standing in the doorway to the kitchen and says, "I beg your pardon?" Bryce jumps in to stop what could be a huge cat fight and says, "Whoa whoa whoa, ladies let's not get carried away. Christie, I brought Angie here because she came forward with the truth about her testimony. She and her daughter need protection here at the safe house as well. She is now a key witness, and they have already made threats on her life." Christie says, "Whatever, I still know what you did with Melvin bitch!" Her daughter looks over at her Mom and says, "What is she talking about Mom?" Angie says, "Don't worry honey it was all in the past." Bryce wants to calm the waters, so he stands up and says, "Listen, we all need to work together like family to put this corruption behind us. Can we all just get along please?" Christie says, "I guess the big picture here is more important at this time." Angie says, "I agree, I am here now to help." Christie says, "I am sorry it's been a long week. I am on edge just a little bit." She looks over at Bryce and says, "Have you heard anything about Greg's DNA yet?" Bryce says, "No not yet, but the warrant was secured, and we are in the process of collecting DNA of the items you let us take. It won't take long." Christie says, "Good, I need to be the first person you tell when you find out. So don't forget that!" Bryce says, "And we still have not found Greg, do you have any idea where he may have ridden off to?" Christie says, "No he usually rides the coast when he goes on a ride. I'd watch for him along those major highways. Heading south to California." Bryce says, "OK, I can't put out an APB just yet but if the DNA hits, we can get outside departments to BOLO." Christie says, "What is BOLO?" Bryce says, "It stands for Be-On-the-Look-Out."

Just then Bryce got a text on his phone. It was Kat and it reads: "We have confirmation. The DNA matches the blood evidence to Greg Flint." Christie sees Bryce looking at his phone and she can't help but wonder if it's a text about Greg. She says, "Bryce can I talk to you in private." Bryce says, "Yes, follow me up to the command room." They go upstairs and the command room is full of security camera monitors that show all rooms and outside angles of the house. Christie says, "Whoa, not much privacy in this house. I'll remember that when I take a shower." Bryce says, "Yeah, in a safehouse you are pretty much a prisoner with a small level of comfort. Anyways, I just received a text from our director of forensics, Kathy Dunbar. She has a match to the DNA." Bryce looks at Christie and she is speechless but is begging him for the results with her eyes. Bryce says, "Christie, it is a match to Greg." She grabs the swivel chair at the desk next to her and collapses into the seat. She tears up and through a sobbing voice says, "You need to find him NOW! Don't let him get away with this Bryce!" Bryce says, "I will put out an APB now and the search will be on! I want to tell you.

This evidence will not be enough to free Melvin. We will need Greg to confess. I will need you to hold it together enough to help us in getting his confession. If he believes you are going to stay with him, he may cooperate with us. Can you help to support him just for a little longer until we get what we need from him? In these situations, the killer always seeks approval from the ones they love." Christie pushes back her tears and says, "I can't even right now! I just need to be alone." She gets up and walks to her bedroom and shuts the door. Bryce can hear her scream into a pillow as he walks back down the stairs. Bryce writes a text back to Kat, it reads: "Get a warrant for Greg's arrest and put out an APB for the capture of Gregory Wilson Flint." Kat texts back: "10-4."

Two hours went by, and Christie hadn't left her room. Bryce is pacing the control room when a call comes into his cell phone. It is Kat. He answers, "Kat, please tell me you have some news." She says, "I do Bryce, but it's not good. They have found Greg and his motorcycle just beyond Portland at the Willamette Valley." Bryce says, "Why is that not good? I need to talk with him ASAP, Christie says she will help in getting him to confess." Kat says, "Bryce he has already confessed. He rode his motorcycle off a cliff near some falls in the Valley and he was dead on arrival at the hospital. His motorcycle jacket had a confession note with the details about Jackie's death. This should be enough to free Melvin and for you to proceed on your other cases." Bryce says, "Thank you Kat, I will break the news to the team here and we will have a lot of work ahead."

Chapter 36

Detective Roberts is sitting at his office at the police station and sees that Bryce Edwards has added a file on Angie VanPatton as a key witness in the Melvin Casey secondary investigation pool. This is when Chief Pavlock walks by and says, "Roberts, we need to talk! Meet me in my office when you have a minute, it is important before you leave that you see me." Jon says, "OK Chief, let me finish this entry log quick and I will stop by." Just as Detective Roberts looks back at his computer an APB alert pops up on his computer screen for Gregory Wilson Flint. He clicks on the APB alert to read that Greg has a warrant for his arrest in a murder that happened in Seattle. He pulls out his phone and decides to call Ben Henke with an update. He starts off by saying, "Ben, I have an update for you, but I can't do it here, I am at the station. Can we meet out at the old Johnson boat warehouse near the ridge?" Ben agrees and says he will bring George to meet him out there. The detective closes his phone, packs up a few things, and heads out quickly to meet with the guys. As soon as he is gone the Chief walks out to see his desk is now empty and says loudly for the cops within ear shot to hear, "Shit, does anyone listen to me around here!"

Detective Roberts pulls into the warehouse drive, parks his car and walks into their usual meeting room. The old Johnson boat warehouse has been abandoned for years, and nobody ever goes down there so it is very secluded. As he looks around in the dark, he looks for at least one light to try and turn on. He can't find any, but Ben Henke pulls up with his car lights shining into the room. He could hear that they had left the car running and the lights continued to shine into the warehouse windows.

Before they exit the car, Detective Roberts hears his phone ping and opens his phone to see a text from Kathy Dunbar. It reads: "Greg's DNA is a match. We have an APB and Warrant out for his arrest. If you run into him, please apprehend him and bring him to the station so Bryce can get him to confess."

Just then the Detective hears two car doors and looks out to see both Ben and George walking up to the entrance. They walk in and Ben says, "OK we are here for an update, are we home free yet?" George just repeats what Ben says and yells, "HOME FREE BABY!" He likes to hear the echo in the large, abandoned buildings. Detective Roberts is in full Detective gear and says to them. Well not quite yet, we have more issues. First off, I need to find out from George what really happened at the Casey household that night!" George says, "What do you mean 10 years ago when I killed Jackie? What are you gonna arrest me now Mr. Detective?" Ben jumps in and says, "First of all you were paid to kill Melvin! When you killed Jackie instead, we had to improvise." Detective Roberts says, "I know all that but the DNA evidence at the scene just matched Greg Flint and there is a nationwide hunt for him tonight!" Ben Henke turns to look directly into George's eyes and says, "Wait, is he telling me I paid you to kill NOBODY! That I gave you 25 grand for nothing!" George says, "I didn't want to tell you guys, I saw the kid there and I just couldn't kill his dad. I didn't even realize his dad wasn't even there and that was just some dude banging his wife!" Detective Roberts says, "Well then what happened!" George said, "I don't know they both started fighting about their affair and I hid in the closet. Next thing I knew the dude was cleaning up blood and screaming. He was outta there and I did the same." Detective Roberts jumps in and says, "Now they have Angie as a witness, she turned herself over to the police today too." When Ben Henke heard this come out of his mouth, he didn't hesitate one second and pulled out his revolver and shot George right in the heart. BANG! Detective Roberts reached for his gun and before he could even pull it out Ben turned and shot him in the chest. BANG! Detective Roberts fell to the ground and Ben knew he was wearing a bulletproof vest, so he walked up and shot him in the head twice. BANG! BANG!

Ben pauses for a moment in silence. With them both dead, and the smoking gun in his hand he knew this was not going to end well for him. His first thought was he could flee from the scene and avoid capture, so he walked out to his running car. He opens the door and sits down in the driver's seat. His revolver is still fresh in his hand. He has never run away from his problems before, but this one is a bigger problem than he has ever seen. He has gone from always being in control to now being totally out of control. With Melvin out of prison, Angie as a key witness, and now two more deaths to cover up he sees no way out. He takes the revolver and turns it on himself ending a 30-year run of corrupt public service.

THE END

Aaron is such a strong character in this book. The story surrounding his memory has sparked a spin-off of Dr. Brian Jaims and his practice. The stories behind Dr. Brian Jaims just come easier. "The Eidetic Evidence," was started in the early 2000s and the timeline of this book ends in 2011. Even though I wrote a lot of it in 2018 and 2019. I kept the original timeline as it was. This leaves Aaron, at the time of publishing in 2025, to be 25 years old. I have thought of writing more stories of Aaron, as an adult, in his own therapy practice or as a detective with his photographic memory solving complex cases in Los Angeles or Chicago (I live close to Chicago Area). We will see where that goes in the future with my new hobby of writing short novels.

Miley is also a strong character in, "The Eidetic Evidence." If you didn't grow up with a strong friend that always had your back, I feel sorry for you. Miley is a great friend. Did she grow up to marry Aaron? This is another thought to cross my mind. I can see her as an entrepreneur, owning multiple businesses or as a CEO of a large corporation. She is so smart and quick-witted. She can warrant a spin-off on her own as a detective as well. Or even as a lawyer defending domestic violence victims. She would be anyone's worse nightmare in a courtroom.

Dr. Blake. Where do I begin? His foresight to know he needed help to get Aaron to the next level in his memory vault was superb. Bringing in Dr. Jaims and connecting him as an old college roommate was something that just felt right to me. Dr. Blake will eventually stop working with Aaron shortly after Aaron started high school. They will remain friends forever, for obvious reasons. In the next Aaron Casey novel, he will be asking Dr. Blake for moral support and advice along the way. I see Dr. Blake being a future character that guides Aaron into seeing things differently. When Aaron is stuck, he calls on Dr. Thomas Blake to help him, "see the light."

Christie is a fireplug. She will begin a new life after Greg's death. It won't be easy for her but with Melvin's release, he will move back into his house, and she will continue to live with him in the house. She will constantly prank him when she can because he held the knowledge of the affair from her for years. Payback was well overdue, and she must find a way to laugh about it by keeping Melvin on his toes with weekly pranks. She goes back to school to finish her teaching degree and becomes an amazing elementary school teacher in Seattle. She is proof that it is never too late in life to start over.

The Sanders Family. Not much has changed for them. They hold on to Miley a little closer each day after this whole situation is over. Mr. Sander's continues to plan his outdoor family vacations; however, on a sad note, the backyard campouts end with what you read in Chapter 13. Insert sad face here. :(

Bryce Edwards leads King County as an amazing District Attorney. He is still the D.A. to this day. He exposed Ben Henke after his death. The reach of that investigation swept far enough to get Chief Pavlock in trouble as well. The Chief resigned and kept his pension, but he will never work in law enforcement ever again.

Melvin Casey. He tried to regain his status on the bar; however, his admission by motion was denied. He now works as a consultant for 5 law firms. His settlement with King County, for his time served, was put into a trust for Aaron and was partially donated to The Jonathan Charity where Mel Casey was voted onto the Board of Directors in 2013. Melvin takes pride in volunteering for the charity that his late wife started many years earlier.

***

Follow the continuation of this series on Facebook. Search for "Dr. Brian Jaims Detective Novels"

You can interact with us there via direct message or with likes and comments. Thank you for your support.

From the Author:

Thank you for reading <u>The Eidetic Evidence</u>. I hope you enjoyed it. Please leave a review for this story at Barnes and Noble's website if you have the time. Stay tuned for Book 2 or what I call (Memory 2). It will follow the Dr. Brian Jaims storyline in <u>The Elicit Evidence</u>. Coming soon to bookshelves near you.